# Seven More Stories

T. Farley is also the author of *The Buffalo and Other Stories*

All characters and events are fictional, except for those in the story "Mother Goes to Mars." Any other resemblance to actual events or people is coincidental.

*Seven More Stories* is written by T. Farley

Copyright 2010 © Thomas Farley

ISBN:1-59330-683-0

Cover design by Elizabeth Farley

# Seven More Stories

✳   ✳   ✳

**T. Farley**

*For Mary Louise*

# Contents

Prodigal Son ...................................................1

Clean Living.................................................13

The Parts Business........................................41

Mother Goes to Mars.....................................63

The Sunset Program.......................................73

Time Traveler ..............................................81

Change.......................................................97

# Prodigal Son

"He should be here."

"Not yet," his wife said, as she glanced at the clock over the sink. "He said it might be after dark—it's only four o'clock."

"The weather's turning bad and he should be here. It's been going bad all day and he should know to start back early."

"I'm sure he's safe, Ed. I think he can handle himself."

"I'm not so sure…" and his voice trailed off as he went out onto the front porch of the cabin. The wind was blowing and overhead he could see the first gray clouds pushing up-canyon from the west. An early season storm out of the Pacific had swept onto land that morning, and forecasters were predicting wind and cold temperatures, possibly even snow.

"I should never have let him go," he said, reentering the cabin.

"You had a choice?" his wife replied. "He goes where he wants."

"But he just got back. You would think he would wait a few days—not take off right away."

"You know how he is. When he decides on something, he does it."

Ed paced from inside the cabin to the porch and back for most of the next hour. At one point, he left the porch and walked the forty or so yards down to the stream and peered up-canyon along the trail. His son wasn't visible. Finally, at a few minutes past five o'clock, he got his pack out of the closet and said, "Kay, I'm going looking for him."

"Now, Ed, are you sure about this?"

"Yes. I want to leave while there is still some light. If he's coming down the trail, I'll run into him. If he's in trouble, I'll have at least a couple of hours of daylight to find him."

"Where will you look for him?"

"Jenks Flat. He said he was headed for Pindel Mountain and Jenks is half way."

"That's five miles from here. You won't be there until after dark. What if he comes back some other way?"

"He won't. He didn't bring a GPS or a map and doesn't know how to use either of them anyway. He'll come back through Jenks where he knows the way."

He was ready in ten minutes. He packed gloves and a hat, five energy bars, some jerky, and two quarts of water. Then he laced up his boots and pulled a windbreaker over his heavy sweater. "I may not be back until late," he told his wife.

She nodded and followed him out onto the front porch. She had a bad feeling about this and as soon as he disappeared up the trail, she walked the ten minutes to the ranger station a quarter mile downstream. She knocked on the screen door of the small residence at the rear.

"Hello, Don. Ed's gone after Jimmy and left ten minutes ago."

"What for? Jimmy's not due back until later."

"You know how Ed is. The weather's turning and he's worried. I just want you to know what's going on."

"Thanks, Kay. I'll give it a couple of hours. If I don't hear from you, I'll be up at your place by, say, eight."

"I hope they're back by then. I'm making a cake and getting ready for tomorrow. Dean should be here soon and it will be nice to have everyone together again," said Kay, scratching Ralph, Don's German shepherd. Don nodded and Kay turned and started back to the cabin.

There was about a thousand feet of elevation gain along the trail from the cabin to Jenks Flat. The trail followed the stream along the bottom of the narrow canyon, progressing on a steady incline, but rose quickly the last half mile. The final hundred yards of trail was a scramble up a very steep slope. Ed moved at a good pace, and covered the first two miles of trail by six o'clock. As he walked along, he was preoccupied by thoughts of his son. Jimmy had always been a concern, ever since he was six and began school. Jimmy had been slow to read and write, and had difficulty pronouncing even the simplest words and being able to form his letters. He printed in an odd, cramped style and would reverse letters or even reverse the order of words in a sentence. He was twelve-years-old before he could put together a simple, three-sentence paragraph.

The other children laughed at Jimmy when he first tried to read out loud in school. Jimmy was sent to another class but not before he was tested, interviewed, and finally examined by specialists sent by the school district. Then Ed had Jimmy removed from school and sent to a private school on the other side of town. Jimmy did not like the new school and acted that way. Before long, the new school asked Jimmy's parents to remove him, and then Ed ran Jimmy through four more schools before Kay was allowed to bring Jimmy home on a trial basis. Kay proceeded to teach Jimmy to read and write herself, but he never became a very good reader nor did he ever write very well. Kay realized early on, however, that Jimmy had a head for math and, it seemed, an excellent memory. Jimmy also liked to draw, so Kay put him in art lessons painting fish and bowls of fruit, though he preferred drawing automobiles, bridges, and buildings. When Jimmy was ten-years-old, Kay was astounded to find a perfect, three-dimensional drawing of a birdcage on the easel in his bedroom. They had seen the birdcage in the window of a shop at the beach two days earlier and Jimmy had pointed it out.

Ed was never very happy that Kay brought Jimmy home for school. And so, every year, Ed had Jimmy undergo a series of tests to measure his academic progress and, every year, Jimmy did poorly on these tests. This angered Ed, and he would have put Jimmy in another school except Kay was opposed to it and Jimmy threatened to run away, which he did—twice. The first time, the police found Jimmy sleeping in the bus station in Phoenix. Jimmy made it further the second time—getting caught sneaking onto a train in Amarillo. Finally, Ed decided Jimmy could stay at home with Kay.

Then Ed was forced out of his position at the investment firm he helped found, negotiated a large settlement so he would never have to work again, and moved to the mountains for what he called "family time." Ed put a trailer on a lot they purchased a quarter mile up from the ranger station, and made plans to build a home adjacent to it. Ed retained an architect but Kay suggested Jimmy draw up some plans, which he did on brown shipping paper. As Kay, Jimmy, and Jimmy's older brother, Dean, all held their tongues as best they could, Ed took a scissors and cut the large porch off the rustic cabin Jimmy designed and taped it onto the front of the chalet-style dwelling the architect designed. The eventual result was a peculiar structure that always attracted the attention of hikers on the trail. But before there was a structure for hikers to notice, Ed and Jimmy had to nail forms together and cement trucks had to strain up the canyon road to pour concrete for the foundation. After the foundation was complete, Ed and Jimmy began to argue in earnest and the project sputtered along until Jimmy finally stormed off. Ed then brought in a contractor from the valley to finish the cabin. Jimmy stayed one more year in the mountains, mostly at the ranger station or on the trail with Don, until Don got him on a fire crew. Jimmy fought fires all over the west for four years, making two hundred and forty dollars a week, and had come home the previous day for his father's birthday. Ed had a talk prepared for Jimmy about Jimmy's future, but Jimmy took off for Mount Pindel the day after arriving. Now Ed found himself trudging up the trail to Jenks Flat rehearsing his talk for Jimmy.

By half past seven o'clock, Ed had gone five miles and was scrambling up the last section of trail near Jenks Flat. Reaching the edge of the flat, he stopped and rested, sitting on a fallen log. He had expected to meet Jimmy on the trail, and reaching Jenks Flat was something he hadn't actually anticipated. It was dusk and the wind was blowing, driving clouds over the low treetops of Jenks Flat. The old-growth cedar and pine had been logged years earlier and now a great thicket of young, slender pines interspersed with brush covered the surface of the flat. Jenks Flat spread out over an area of almost two square miles and had something of a desolate feel to it, even in daylight, though he had been here only twice before. He hadn't enjoyed either of his previous visits and now, in the failing light, Jenks Flat seemed even bleaker than he remembered.

Ed rested a few minutes and then got up to push on. He felt some urgency, remembering a fork in the trail ahead where he had trouble previously. The trail traversed the south edge of Jenks Flat before crossing a stream flowing from the north, after which the trail split into two branches. It would be important to find the stream before it became totally dark, because there was a peculiar jog in the trail after it crossed the stream where one had to bear hard left to find the correct branch of the trail. He had missed this jog the two previous times he had been at Jenks Flat, traveling on a mile or so each time before sensing something amiss and turning to retrace his steps. This time, though, Ed got out his flashlight and carefully negotiated the jog, making sure he found the correct branch of the trail. He did this as the clouds above him abruptly broke and a bright moon appeared to the east. The wind slackened and he clicked off his flashlight.

Ed paused, feeling energized. He had gone almost six miles in three hours and the worst of the trail was behind him. The trail would stay mostly flat from here and it looked like there would even be a bit of moonlight to guide him. He felt certain he would encounter his son at any moment. He opened his pack and drank some water. He also ate two energy bars made of compressed grain and fiber bound together by a sweet, green, sticky substance. Then, as quickly as the clouds had broken earlier, they suddenly closed. The wind picked up again. Then it began to snow.

Ed felt confident as he started down the trail with his flashlight. Despite the wind and snow, he was warm and now relaxed and his son was sure to be just ahead of him, about to be encountered on the trail. He would scold his son, wag his finger good-naturedly, and then embrace him and walk him safely home. These were comforting thoughts as he continued along the trail.

At ten minutes before eight o'clock, Jimmy opened the porch door of the cabin and greeted his mother. Dean drove up a minute or two later and there was a reunion of sorts, at least until Kay asked Jimmy if he had seen his father on the trail. Jimmy replied that he had not come down the trail, but had traversed around to the north along Davis Ridge and dropped down one of the tributary canyons to intersect the trail just upstream of the cabin. Then Don knocked on the porch door and there was a conference, after which Don returned to the ranger station to get Betty. Betty was the mule and she was to be the third member of their group, along with Don and Jimmy. Ralph would go with them also, as the fourth member, because he was the sniffer. Dean was overweight and had a sinus infection and couldn't sniff at all, so he would remain at the cabin with his mother. As the group prepared to leave, Kay decided it might be a good time for her to pray.

At Jenks Flat, Ed was moving easily along the trail toward Pindel Mountain. The trail traversed the interior of Jenks Flat, winding through brush and pine. Snow was falling at intervals, but the moon sent off a faint glow through the streaks of cloud passing overhead. Ed periodically clicked his light on, and he generally continued along what seemed to be an opening in the brush that he thought defined the trail. After forty-five minutes, Ed became uneasy as, by now, he should have reached the far edge of Jenks Flat. He soon halted and paused a few moments, slowly sweeping his light across the terrain around him. The light could find only brush and thin pine trees. Ed looked down and thought he could see the trail at his feet. Finally, he decided to continue with his light turned on so his son might see it.

After another half hour, Ed knew he was somehow off track. He was still surrounded by brush and pine, and again he swept his flashlight around him. Pointing the light downward, he was surprised to find fresh footprints in the thin dusting of snow. His heart quickened and he called out for Jimmy, but there was no response. He followed the footprints for several yards, but then noticed they were going in the direction he was going. He stopped and looked at both sets of prints. He realized both sets were his own. He had been walking in a circle—for how long, he wasn't sure.

Ed began to backtrack. He also worried—what had happened to Jimmy? If he could not find his way through Jenks Flat at night, certainly Jimmy couldn't either. He had a sickening feeling that Jimmy was lost, and he knew his son had not brought heavy clothing. Nevertheless, he backtracked for half an hour until he spotted new footprints—this time in thicker snow. He called again for Jimmy and waited; then he looked carefully at these new prints and realized, once again, that they were his own. He quickly concluded that not only had he been walking in some sort of circle, but possibly more than one circle. Shining his flashlight all around him, the beam encountered nothing but brush and thin pine. He now felt cold.

Ed wandered for another hour through Jenks Flat, and then his light gave out. He took off his pack and got out his gloves, then sat down on the gloves with his back against a small tree to rest. The snow was falling more heavily and the clouds were now thick enough to block the moonlight. He concluded that he probably had enough clothing to survive the night, if necessary, but that Jimmy probably didn't. This thought preoccupied him as he rested.

Ed felt something suddenly warm and wet on his face—and he opened his eyes to find Ralph. Ralph was eagerly sweeping his large, wet tongue across Ed's face, and Ed couldn't help but notice something rank on Ralph's breath. Twenty yards away, Don was bringing up Betty and just behind Don and Betty came Jimmy, smiling excitedly. Don wasn't smiling and Betty seemed agitated, her ears laid back. Ralph continued to run his tongue across Ed's face.

"Thank God we found you," said Jimmy as he lurched past Don and the mule. "That Ralph is a smart dog—he found you even in this thicket." Jimmy squat down and embraced his father, pressing him tight against him. "Oh—you're pretty cold! We've got a stove to make some tea—you need to warm up!"

Ed was so cold that he had trouble speaking. He remained propped against the thin pine tree where he had sat down earlier. "What time is it?" he suddenly blurted.

"Just after two," replied Don, retrieving the stove from the pack on the mule.

"I must have fallen asleep."

"I believe so—you're lucky we found you," Don said.

"You're safe Jimmy? Don found you?"

"I didn't find him—he was at the cabin," Don said.

"At the cabin? How did you get to the cabin? I went up the trail and never saw you," said Ed.

"I didn't come down the trail. I traversed around the north side of the canyon along Davis Ridge and came down Tubbs Creek. It enters the canyon just upstream from the cabin."

"Jimmy said he might be late," Don said, as a reminder. "He was back at the cabin just before eight."

Ed was suddenly agitated. "You really took a chance! You didn't have a GPS or a map and you have no sense of direction—you took a big risk making a trip like that!"

"Jimmy gets around just fine," Don interrupted sharply. "He has no trouble reading a map and usually knows exactly where he is—I know because I taught him."

"Oh, you taught him! Just when did you teach him?"

"While you finished your cabin—after you ran him off. He had to have somewhere to go and I brought him with me. Taught him maps. Taught him also about the mountains and the critters—bears and cats and the deer and such. Did he tell you about the award he got on the fire crew? He's their best navigator—always knows where he is. That's how he saved that fella with the broken leg. Why don't you give him some credit for once? You always run him down."

Ed was quiet. Then he began to cry. Then he was sobbing and breathing hard, gulping for air. Jimmy cradled him and Ralph came over again to lick his face.

"Damn it, Ed, cut it out!" Don said. "Get a grip on yourself—you're balling like a girl!"

"Don't say anything more, grandpa," said Jimmy. "It's been a long night. Is the water boiling yet?"

"Just about," Don growled. "Tea in two minutes."

"You didn't have to say that," Ed said to Don as he drank the tea. "You didn't have to say that in front of Jimmy. You never approved of anything I ever did. You never thought anything I did was important."

Don said nothing and drank his tea. He then got an apple out of Betty's pack and fed it to Betty.

They were on the move by three o'clock. Ed insisted on walking and so he was placed between Jimmy and Don, with Ralph running up ahead and Betty bringing up the rear. By five o'clock, Ed was exhausted and on the back of Betty. They had two miles more to the cabin when Betty laid her ears down again and halted on the trail. Don said something to her and she snorted. Then Ed dismounted, and Don again got out the stove.

"I've got some instant coffee," Don said. "Let's warm up a bit before we finish. The cold is bothering Betty."

Don made the coffee and then pulled a flask from Betty's pack. He opened the flask and poured some of it into each of the three cups of coffee. Then he reached again into Betty's pack, took out an apple and cored it, and poured some of the flask's contents into the hole in the apple. "This should get her home," said Don. "Betty needs another apple—but this time with some kick. She's getting old—like me," said Don as he fed the apple to Betty. Then he splashed some of the flask's contents onto Ralph's tongue. Ralph yelped and spun twice. He then shook himself and came back to Don, sniffing for more.

"Anyone for an energy bar?" inquired Ed. "I've got two more." He had opened one of his compressed grain and fiber bars, the ones bound with the green, sticky substance.

"I don't believe so. Looks like something that came out of the back of Betty," Don said.

Ed began laughing. Then Jimmy started laughing and finally Don. Soon they were all laughing hard. Finishing their coffee, they all felt better and Betty's ears were standing back up.

Then Don began, "You're right, Ed, I never gave you much credit. I never understood what you did or how you made your money. Seemed like gambling to me—hedge funds and options and selling long and short and such. But seven years ago, after your mother died, I took your advice on some stocks. I spent a lot of money when your mother got sick, and I took what I had left over and invested it. The stocks did pretty well—like you said they would. I've sold most of them and I'm in good shape now. It will make a difference—thanks for your help."

"Oh, you're welcome. I had no idea you bought stocks. You should tell me which ones you have left—I might be able to help you there."

"Well, I'll show you when we get back. I haven't told anyone this, but I've put in my papers. I'm three years past retirement age and they want me to go."

"Oh, I'm sorry. What are you going to do now?"

"I've got my eye on the old Stuart place. It's run down but I've talked to them and I can get it cheap. You and Jimmy can help me with renovations, but maybe you can also look over the paperwork. I'd like to get the papers settled this coming week."

"Glad to do it. I'll look at both the papers and your stock."

"Thanks. And happy birthday, son—I just remembered."

"Happy birthday!" echoed Jimmy.

"Thanks—both of you," replied Ed. "Thanks for coming out for me."

They covered the last two miles of trail in less than an hour. Ed took the lead, then came Jimmy, and finally Don with Betty behind him. Ralph, as always, loped back and forth along the trail ahead of them. Dean was watching for them from the cabin porch, and he called to Kay when they came into view. Kay ran down to meet them on the trail, Dean lagging behind. The sun was up and the clouds were clearing and it looked like it would be a nice day.

"I see you got him back," Kay eventually said to Jimmy, off to the side.

"Yep, found him up on Jenks Flat."

"Not the same place as last time?" inquired Dean, coming over.

"No. He found a new place to get lost."

"How's grandpa taking it?" asked Dean.

"Good, I think, real good. They had a talk. Things should be better between them," gestured Jimmy toward his father and grandfather, who were standing next to Betty. Ed had taken Betty's reins and was shouting directions to some hikers on the trail, a finger pointing up-canyon toward Jenks flat.

"Maybe you could get grandpa to teach dad about maps," said Dean to Jimmy. "Or teach him yourself. Then you won't have to do this again."

"Crazy old fool," said Kay, grinning. "Look at him over there talking to those hikers—thinks he's a real mountain man."

"Let's get some cake," said Dean, rubbing his stomach. "I'm hungry."

# Clean Living

It was time to go. He made a final walk through the house, checking again the doors and windows on the lower floor. Everything was secure, as it had been earlier that morning when he checked the first time. Pausing in the foyer to turn off the porch light, he then stepped over to the large, floor-length mirror to check himself. His dark wool trousers remained clean and crisp, a good match to his tweed jacket. He typically avoided wool—it reminded him of winters in West Virginia when he was growing up. But the wool of his jacket and trousers was a lightweight blend, and the trousers and jacket seemed to align his wide hips and sloping, narrow shoulders into a straight, if thick, frame. He decided he looked somewhat sophisticated—his large, graying head contrasting nicely with the dark slacks and tweed. He had noticed the president of his company wearing wool at a planning meeting three weeks earlier, and it was then that he decided he liked wool.

He left the hallway and entered the kitchen, pulling a box of unopened mail from a cabinet and setting it on the counter, so he would see it when he returned home. He paused by the door connecting the house to the garage, scanning the kitchen a final time. Everything seemed to be in order. The sink was clean and empty—he had washed four stacks of glasses that morning. The counters and appliances gleamed and shined—he finally wiped them of dust last night before going to bed.

He had been annoyed by the dust and stacks of glasses in the sink. He thought his wife should be home to look after the house.

Entering the garage, he found it orderly and with everything in its proper place. He got into his car and used the remote to open the vertical door, and then backed out. He pressed the remote again, and the garage door closed. He backed down the drive to the street, where he paused to scan the house and yard. Everything on the outside seemed to be in good order. He liked this house and the thick white columns that bracketed the front porch. There were six columns—three on each side—and they gleamed in the morning sun. His wife thought the columns were overstated and too large for the house, but he liked them. He thought they gave the house stature.

The drive to San Antonio would take a little over three hours, but he was leaving early in case of traffic or car trouble or some other delay. If it looked like he would arrive early as planned, he would stop for coffee and the restroom before covering the last ten miles. He was actually looking forward to the drive and then the afternoon with his wife's brother's family. They always put on a big Christmas spread with everyone sitting down to a nice meal in the early afternoon. He would arrive before noon and visit briefly before they ate; then leave by four o'clock and be home again after seven. The three hour drive each way would give him time to think.

He had been at the office until five the previous afternoon. It had been just he and Alberto going over some last figures, and he left Alberto to finalize a presentation he would be giving the first week of the new year. Alberto e-mailed the presentation to him just after seven o'clock, and he had it carefully reviewed by eight. There were no errors and he called Alberto at home to confirm this, and also to wish Alberto and his wife a Merry Christmas, but there had been no answer. He also had been unable to reach Alberto's cell phone, and this had irritated him.

The irritation quickly passed. As he had put down the phone, a group of carolers began at the neighboring house. He had been expecting this and left his desk and study to go sit in his leather chair at the front window near the door. He had closed the curtains earlier and dimmed the lights in the foyer, but the porch light had been turned on to attract the carolers. This was his third holiday season in the house, and his wife offered cakes and cider to the carolers on the two previous occasions. He was by himself this year and had nothing to offer the carolers, but he still had waited for them.

He had always enjoyed Christmas music. It was not so much the lyrics, but the music itself that he found appealing. So he sat quietly in his chair as the carolers drew up and began, first with "Joy to the World," followed by "Silent Night," and "We Wish You a Merry Christmas." When the carolers finished, he could hear them shuffling about briefly on the walkway and then a few low voices, but soon they were gone. He then waited for them to begin again at the next house before reaching for the remote on the table beside him and turning on the stereo. He kept the volume low as more Christmas music poured out of the speakers. He had gone down to the mall earlier in the week and purchased this music. There were no words—just an orchestra. He also had set out most of the elaborate nativity set his wife had purchased years earlier, and the camels and shepherds and wise men put him in a festive mood. He had sat there for half an hour, the music soaring over him.

The first hour of the drive to San Antonio passed quickly. As expected, traffic was light on the interstate and there were no delays. He had plenty to think about, as the coming year would bring significant change. He had been appointed a vice president before Thanksgiving and would assume his new position in January. He would have his own division and an expanded staff, but Alberto was moving to a new job and he would have to find a competent replacement. Already, he had a certain young woman in mind and had discreetly approached her about the job. She was receptive, and he had set in motion a plan to extract her from her current supervisor. She was a very bright, hard-working woman who seemed to grasp the business particularly well and had worked well with Alberto—Alberto even recommending her. Her gender would improve the diverseness of his staff, particularly now that Alberto was moving on. She was also homely and could even be considered unattractive, and he thought she might even be religious. He considered these positive characteristics—she was unlikely to get entangled in office romance or politics. She seemed to be the type who would just work and follow directions and not become overly inquisitive or gregarious like Alberto. Alberto was very smart—maybe even smarter than he was—but Alberto's shrewdness and sociability had always worried him.

He checked his watch and then the time on the dashboard clock. They were four minutes apart and this suddenly bothered him. He had another hour to go before stopping to get coffee and use the restroom. He would adjust the dashboard clock then. Now he had more things to think about.

He planned to go to the office tomorrow morning while the building was quiet and empty. The corner of the seventh floor was being renovated for him, and he was monitoring its progress. The contractor was supposed to have men there working, and his appearance and questions on a holiday weekend would hopefully serve as another goad for the contractor to finish on schedule. He had insisted the corner be finished quickly, so he could get his personal staff in place by the end of the year. Three of his staff would be inherited from his predecessor, and he would add four of his own. Of the three he would inherit, one would be useful to him but the other two wouldn't. The two that wouldn't be useful had been asking questions and making suggestions. This would soon be rectified—he had little tolerance for overly inquisitive staff members with ideas of their own, particularly holdovers. As a new vice president, he intended to make changes and put his mark on the organization quickly.

After another hour, he was pulling his automobile off the interstate and making for a truck stop on the service road. He was familiar with the place and it was always open. It had separate stations for cars and trucks and a food mall where he could get his coffee. He replaced a third of a tank of gas before going inside. Most shops in the food mall were closed for Christmas, but the coffee shop was always open and he sat down with a cup after using the restroom. He would now spend ten minutes or so preparing for his wife's brother's family. The family would be polite and cheerful, but he expected a few probing questions or at least a comment or two. He had his answers prepared, but sat and reviewed them again anyway.

Twenty minutes later, he pulled up at his brother-in-law's house. There were five cars and a tow truck parked on the street out front, and three more cars and a tow truck on the driveway. The house was a long, rambling structure spread across a large lot. His brother-in-law had been in it for over twenty years and the place had a comfortable, casual feel about it. There were bicycles on the lawn and a few toys on the driveway, but he was able to fit his car behind the tow truck on the driveway in a slot before the street. The two oldest boys were on the driveway next to the garage, tending to turkeys frying in two vats.

"Hello, there! Happy holidays to you!"

"Hello, Uncle Mort! Merry Christmas!" both men replied. "You had a safe drive? No trouble coming up?"

"None at all."

"Dad's been looking for you—he comes out and checks every ten minutes or so."

"Then I'll go look for him. See you boys after a while."

As he approached the front door, it opened and there was Frank. Frank was short, reddish, and wiry. He wore red and green plaid pants, a green vest over a white shirt, and a maroon beret with "Garcia Towing" imprinted in gold on the side. "There he is! Right on time! Merry Christmas, Mort!"

"Hello, Frank! How's the tow truck business?"

"Busy as ever—I've got more business than I know what to do with. I just bought four more trucks—that brings it to thirty-four. How's the oil business and how was the drive up?"

"Both good, very good."

"Come on in. Cat is just about ready and we'll eat soon—just another few minutes for the turkeys."

As Mort entered the house, Cat emerged from the kitchen and the two embraced. Mort liked Cat and found her easy to talk to. She was an attractive woman who still had her shape, even after eight children. "So nice of you to come," Cat said, "I wish Jen could have made it, but I understand the situation. I hope being a temporary bachelor hasn't been too hard on you."

"Oh no, I've been managing. I can be fairly self-reliant."

"Well, I know Jen wishes she could be here. I talked to her last night and she said she was going to miss us."

"She'll be home soon enough. Becky is nearly back to her old self and won't need her mother much longer. Jen belongs at home—Becky has to get on with her life."

"And how is Larry? We haven't heard much of him."

"Larry rotated back to the states just after Thanksgiving. He's staying over at Fort Benning with two of his buddies for Christmas."

"Well, it sounds like everything is as good as it could be. I hope the new year brings blessings for all of us."

The house was full of people. Frank got Mort a glass of wine and then brought Mort around to greet everyone. Mort was soon discussing football with two of Frank's neighbors, followed by a second discussion about the governor's election with Frank's brother. Mort was then brought up to date on the towing business by Frank's two oldest sons, who had brought the turkeys inside, after which Mort found himself fielding a number of questions about the price of gasoline. Mort greeted each of Frank's four daughters, but didn't talk long with the oldest two. The oldest daughter was an attorney and the next oldest was a psychiatrist, and conversations with them sometimes strayed into unpredictable territory or ended in an argument.

Then, as was the custom, three long tables were placed end to end in the living room so everyone could sit together. The living room was large, and even with the tables put together, there was still space for chairs and three sofas along the side. Within a few minutes, Frank was summoning everyone to the table. It took a while for everyone to be seated, and then Frank asked each person at the table to offer a brief prayer or word of thanks. Mort always dreaded this part because the younger children and the grandchildren, in particular, could run on and on until either Frank or one of the mothers prodded them to finish. Mort had come to eat and he wanted to get on with it.

As the prayers proceeded, Mort found himself counting heads at the table. All eight of Frank's children had made it, and all seven grandchildren, and two of Frank's brothers. Including spouses, five cousins, six neighbors, himself, and what looked like two derelicts from a men's shelter, Mort counted thirty-four people. He laughed suddenly, for it occurred to him that there was one guest for every tow truck that Frank owned. Some of the others glanced at him, but the prayers continued.

Finally, they were ready to eat. Frank got up from one end of the table and began passing down a large platter of turkey. Cat stood at the other end of the table and sent down a platter of ham. Bowls and baskets of vegetables, rolls, and sauces were positioned at strategic places along the table, and these were passed around in loops of six or seven people. Within ten minutes, everyone had a full plate of food. Then, with everyone adequately provisioned, previous conversations were reinvigorated or new ones commenced.

Mort had been placed at one corner of the table, with Frank to his left and one of Frank's oldest boys to the right. Mort's place at the table had been determined in advance by Frank and Cat, based on prior Christmas incidents. At the Christmas meal two years earlier, Mort had sat next to Frank and Cat's eighth child, a six-year-old boy who lost his grip and dumped the gravy boat in Mort's lap. It wasn't the loud expletive from Mort that shocked everyone so much as the "stupid, clumsy kid" comment that immediately followed. Cat had jumped up, sputtering and flushed, but Frank was up quicker and turned her into the kitchen before she could get out a word. Then last year the seventh child, Stanley, slumped his food-smeared face onto Mort's shoulder when he had a seizure at the table. This time there was no expletive from Mort, but the phrase "dumb kid" was uttered and, as Frank tried to rise, his two oldest sons managed to pin him to his chair. Then everyone watched in horror as Frank grabbed a wine bottle from the table and hurled it at Mort. Cat intercepted it mid-air, mainly because she had played catcher on the softball team in college, and returned the bottle safely to the table. This seventh child, Stanley, had spent ten minutes too long in the birth canal with insufficient oxygen and was, in fact, something of a "dumb kid." Cat cradled Stanley until his seizure ended, and then she and Mort and later Frank got together and went over everything. This year, a new seating arrangement had been adopted.

Mort and Jen argued almost the entire drive home after the "dumb kid" remark. Mort and Jen didn't usually argue because Mort discouraged it, but Jen wouldn't let the incident with Stanley drop. Actually, this argument turned out to be a continuation of another dispute that originated several years earlier. Shortly after Stanley's birth, when it was first determined that things weren't right with Stanley, Mort had commented offhandedly that maybe Stanley's birth would convince Frank and Cat to stop having children. Jen was bothered by the comment but didn't say anything until a few months later, after Mort expressed exasperation when Cat announced at another family gathering that she was pregnant with their eighth child. "Can't they control themselves?" Mort had said on the drive home. "You should say something to your brother—they're breeding like stupid Mexicans over there. And they can barely keep up with what they already have—those children are always running around and getting into something—falling out of trees or breaking windows or bringing home some stray dog or cat."

"There is nothing wrong with that family," Jen had retorted. "They're a fine family and have fine children." But Jen soon realized that there was something more bothering her about Mort's remarks, tied to something that had occurred many years earlier. At Becky's birth, when the umbilical cord had been found wrapped around Becky's neck, there had been a brief, frantic scramble by the doctor to cut it, and Jen had been sterilized. It was a difficult pregnancy, Jen had been sedated for the delivery, and Mort decided the umbilical cord incident required decisive action. Jen had not agreed to Mort's original plan for two children—hopefully a boy and a girl—and despite additional negotiations with Mort, the issue had remained unsettled. Still, Mort had extracted consent from Jen that in the event a medical situation warranted it, something would be done to prevent further pregnancies, and this had been communicated to the doctor. Mort decided the umbilical cord incident provided the appropriate medical opportunity, and so the doctor was instructed to make sure Jen would never conceive again.

When Mort finally told Jen that she could never become pregnant again, she became despondent and stayed that way until Mort took her to a psychiatrist. The psychiatrist prescribed medication, and Jen took the medication for five years. In the summer of the sixth year, Jen and the children went to live with Cat and Frank while Mort was out of the country on a temporary assignment. Jen found religion that summer at the church Frank and Cat attended and got off the drugs, but then Mort returned and got religion and Jen went back on drugs. Mort did not like Jen's religion and found another church, or at least a meeting hall, where people would gather. There was no actual service or worship, just a ring of chairs and sober discussions about various spiritual or philosophical topics among a group of fifteen or twenty people. There was also childcare for Larry and Becky. Mort brought Jen to these meetings for over a year until one night, Larry and another boy beat a third boy nearly senseless. Larry was no longer welcome at childcare, so Mort no longer brought Jen to the meetings. Jen did not like the meetings anyway, and

Mort recommended that she just stick with the drugs. The drugs made Jen compliant, but they also made her anxious and nervous if she took too many. But most of the time Jen was compliant, if not lethargic, and Mort wrote up lists of chores to keep her busy and make sure the housekeeping got done. Mort also brought her to the psychiatrist every few months to get new prescriptions. This had been the arrangement for years and the house remained orderly and clean.

Christmas lunch went on for more than two hours. Several discussions proceeded around the table at once, with both adults and children entering and exiting them at various intervals. There were more discussions about football and the towing business, new discussions about the weather and the past hurricane season, and finally a spirited debate about the upcoming governor's election. The women started their own discussion about children's books, got briefly involved with the men on football, set off on a side debate about the new styles in hats, and finally rejoined the men to discuss the governor's election. Then, as was the Thanksgiving custom when the meal seemed to be drawing to a close and the adults were leaned back in their chairs with coffee or a last glass of wine, Frank was pressed to recount his story of how he got started in the tow truck business. As Frank always described it, this was actually a story about love and the tow truck business or, more accurately, about Zen and love and the tow truck business. No one, not even the regulars, ever seemed to tire of hearing the story—except Mort, who was bored after hearing it the first time fourteen years earlier.

So Frank began the story, starting with his last semester of college and a project he had to complete for his degree in philosophy. The project consisted of recruiting five other students to take a seminar on Zen meditation that Frank would co-teach with one of his professors. Frank quickly rounded up four students, because he was a good talker, but had trouble finding the fifth. The fifth was supposed to be Cat's roommate, but Cat's roommate lost interest after the first meditation session. Frank came looking for Cat's roommate in the dormitories after she failed to appear for the second session, and encountered Cat instead. They got to talking and there was an immediate attraction between the two, even though Cat had no interest in Zen meditation. Frank, however, was persistent.

Frank soon learned that Cat's full name was Catalina Maria Garcia, the last of six daughters born to Armando and Lucy Garcia. Armando and Lucy were from Mexico, and had made a life and six children in Texas. Armando started out as a laborer, and was an ox of a man who worked hard and could save money. After five years, Armando bought Lucy an old bread truck, which she parked at gas stations and from which she sold tamales. When they weren't in school, the six daughters spent their time in the bread truck cooking and selling tamales with their mother. After another five years, Armando bought his first tow truck when he hurt his back and could no longer work as a laborer. Seven years later, Armando had seven tow trucks—each with an image of Our Lady of Guadalupe painted on the doors—and a thriving business, but no son to inherit it. Then, an improbable alliance began to take shape when Armando's and Lucy's youngest daughter, Catalina, met up with Frank who wanted to teach her Zen meditation.

Armando was horrified when he first met Frank. It was at a birthday party for one of Cat's sisters, and Armando found Frank to be the skinniest, hairiest, and palest white guy that he had ever seen in huarache sandals. Armando even asked Lucy if she thought Frank was an albino, though he couldn't quite come up with this term himself and one of the daughters had to whisper it to him. Frank soon came over and introduced himself to Armando, which was initially uneventful until Frank began talking about Zen meditation. One of the six daughters had to explain to Armando what Zen meditation was, and when Frank went on to explain that Zen could liberate Catalina from many of the quaint, archaic ideas and customs she seemed to be burdened with, three of the six daughters thought Armando would have a stroke. Instead, the red-faced Armando wheeled back abruptly and, with a clenched left fist, attempted to liberate Frank from his head. But Frank stepped aside quickly, having sensed something amiss, and Lucy and all six daughters then intervened and order was restored.

But Cat liked Frank and Frank couldn't think of anything but Cat. So Armando eventually realized that Frank would have to be reckoned with. When Frank finally proposed and Cat insisted Frank ask her father for permission to marry, Armando made a series of demands. The first was that Frank become Catholic, the second that Frank actually get a job, and the third was more of a threat—Armando swore he would kill Frank if he was ever unfaithful or broke his daughter's heart. Frank then decided Zen meditation wasn't all it was cracked up to be, took up Armando's offer to drive one of his tow trucks, and wondered if he should buy a gun.

Frank soon completed a demanding six-month training assignment driving one of Armando's tow trucks, during which he conclusively demonstrated to everyone that he was mechanically inept. Armando then figured Frank must have talent elsewhere, so he moved Frank into the office as a dispatcher, where he spent another six months. At the end of the first six months, Frank no longer wore sandals—having broken the big toe on his right foot with a dropped crowbar when he was winching up a '68 Chevelle. Frank also had trimmed his long, pale blond hair—after most of it was first severed in the winch of his tow truck three weeks before the toe and crowbar incident. Frank quickly discovered that he liked going to the Catholic church, particularly when Armando insisted on picking him up on Sunday mornings. After a year of working for Armando and going to church with him, Lucy, and Catalina, the Zen in Frank dissipated and something else began to take over. Part of this something else was an entrepreneurial spirit, and within five years there were seventeen tow trucks in the Garcia Towing fleet, a satellite office in Waco, the first three children born to Frank and Cat, and Armando and Lucy retired to the beach at Corpus Christi. As luck would have it, Frank had a nose for money and business, he liked being Catholic, and he and Cat were in love.

As Frank was finishing up his story, Mort glanced again at his watch. When Cat and some of the older children got up to begin clearing the table, Mort uncharacteristically got up to help. Mort was gone within the half hour. Cat and Frank came outside to see him off, wishing him a safe trip home. Mort was happy to get away and congratulated himself on departing a little early. He was also pleased the visit had gone smoothly. He had been initially apprehensive when Frank called to invite him, but quickly realized that his absence might stoke concern and speculation about Becky's condition and the absence of Jen. So he had made a point of coming, even calling Cat a week earlier to express his anticipation. Mort knew that he had only to eat, be polite, and watch himself around the smaller children. He had handled all of this quite adequately and even enjoyed the visit.

As Mort drove home, his thoughts turned again to work. Though he had finally made vice president, he was in a vulnerable position. He was succeeding his boss, who had been named a corporate officer, but the organization he was inheriting was on the verge of collapse. He should know—he had run most of it himself during the previous six years as general manager, and he was acquainted with all the problems. Costs were creeping up, production was on the verge of a precipitous decline, and only by luck had a total collapse of the division been averted. This luck had consisted of two events—the discovery of a large, new oil pool and then a tanker collision. The new oil pool came about when his boss overturned his decision to pull funding for the exploratory well that would find the new pool—her decision a surprise to him because she had already demonstrated an aversion to risk even stronger than his own. He had been trying to shut down exploratory drilling in the division since he became general manager, and a series of exploratory failures had almost ensured his success. But there was this one last well to drill and it held an odd appeal for his boss, particularly after a presentation by Alberto, and she wanted to proceed with it. The well was an unexpected success and this first well, together with additional production from subsequent wells, stabilized the division's production for three years.

Then, two Septembers ago, a tanker plowed through the company's main offshore production hub, toppling four platforms and mangling all the interconnected piping. This resulted in the stoppage of over half the division's oil and gas production for seven months, but also provided an excuse for not meeting two years' worth of production targets set for his division. It was now sixteen months since the tanker collision and production was fully restored, but forecasts indicated production was again on the cusp of a precipitous decline. The new oil pool discovery, and then the tanker collision, had delayed the onset of this decline just long enough for his boss to be promoted, leaving him, as her successor, to contend with the result.

He originally had not thought much of his boss—dismissing her as just another over-promoted skirt with good social skills and a gender advantage. She had been named vice president at the same time he had been appointed general manager, but he quickly discovered that she was a sharp, shrewd woman with a nose for advancement and a gift for deception. He was aware that she had recommended him as her successor, probably to insure that the legacy of the division would be firmly associated with him. She had seen the reports forecasting the imminent production collapse, and he suspected she wanted to make sure any failure would cling to him rather than her.

So, Mort was inheriting a failing division and the significance of this wasn't lost on him or some others in the company. He had thirty-two years with the firm and had worked hard and planned carefully for his upward ascent. Still, he lagged behind the best of his peers and there was talk among the ranks that this was a sunset promotion—or his last before being forced to retire. His organization was in trouble and would likely be combined with another division unless he could increase production and bring about growth. So, one of the first things he did after his appointment to vice president was have Alberto initiate a complete review of his organization—both of the part he had previously controlled but also parts he hadn't controlled. Alberto had been gathering and analyzing data since Thanksgiving, and several promising ideas had emerged. Alberto was good with numbers and would look at data from different angles and in different combinations, much as he himself had done earlier in his career. In fact, spreadsheets and the advent of the computer were what first gave Mort the edge to begin his upward climb in the company. As an engineer, Mort had a natural affinity for numbers and precision, but he lacked imagination and could never quite anticipate or adapt a new idea or concept the way some of his peers did. He also avoided taking risks, making only those decisions that seemed to have almost no chance of failure. With a computer, however, he found that he could mitigate risk and boil every decision down to an analysis of numbers. By analyzing numbers and identifying trends and relationships, he usually got pointed in the right direction and often to the very threshold of an idea or decision where even he could usually make that last clumsy, unsure, leap. He decided early on that imagination and risk-taking were overrated—all that was needed was data, some software, and a computer.

Mort was able to rise upward in the company this way for almost twenty years, based mainly on knowing what certain numbers meant and on what certain trends of numbers indicated. He avoided taking chances and was predictable, always delivering on what was asked of him. He mastered the numbers of every unit he managed, could show these numbers on simple and orderly graphs and charts, and developed the belief that knowledge of these numbers and being predictable with his numbers was the surest route to the top. Mort became adept at navigating internal politics—avoiding disputes with peers unless he was sure he could win them, doing favors for other managers that he knew would have to be repaid, and always covering his mistakes—and also carefully managed his personal life. Other managers described Mort as being like teflon or one of those non-stick cooking sprays—Mort wouldn't hesitate to burn an employee if that employee crossed him, but he always managed to stay clean himself with nothing unpleasant or nasty adhering to him.

At the same time Mort was pushing upward in the company, a group of his peers was doing likewise. Some of them had caught on to what Mort was doing, or had separately developed some variation of it themselves. A few had advanced by other methods, often because of a law degree or some other particular expertise, and sometimes they had been assisted by gender or race. But there was also a small group of what Mort considered unconventional individuals, a group not specifically focused on numbers and spreadsheets, and he had always harbored a vague uneasiness about them. They were an aggressive and, it seemed to him, an often eccentric and undisciplined group, with nearly all of them very bold or at least possessing a certain confidence about them. They were typically quite active in meetings—making recommendations, exchanging opinions and arguing, even advocating specific courses of action. They often did this without adequate analysis and supporting data—based more on gut reaction or intuition—and Mort had resented that this was tolerated. The size of this group had diminished over time—several careers had already flamed-out due to some rash decision, failed strategy, or serious misadventure of a personal nature. But the few that remained had the ear of senior management, and he monitored these individuals carefully. Five years ago, one of these had been named president of his company, a year after Mort was made a general manager. This new president wanted change and growth and had set aggressive goals. Mort had found himself in a predicament, having little vision or strategy to achieve the goals that this president, and then his own boss, demanded. Mort's focus was usually on the present or even backwards-looking—solidifying his reputation as being steady, knowledgeable, predictive, and reliable. But the new president was interested in growth and the future and began to push in that direction.

Fortunately, when Mort was promoted to general manager, he inherited Alberto. At first he didn't care for Alberto and could barely tolerate him, but Mort soon discovered that Alberto was very bright and had a grasp of the business not usually encountered in someone at such an early stage in his career. Alberto turned out to be very good with numbers and spreadsheets, was politically adept, and a savvy negotiator. Alberto's strongest attributes, however, were his vision and business sense, along with a nose for taking intelligent risks. And so, just as spreadsheets and numbers had earlier provided Mort with a ride upward in the company, Mort recognized that Alberto's vision and business intuition could be ridden upward as well. And he did ride them upward, for six years, keeping Alberto carefully focused on the various goals set for his division. During those six years Alberto identified new technologies, recommended new engineering and business practices to stabilize and improve production, and became an advocate for those few unique projects that seemed to promise large rewards relative to the amount of risk involved—one of these projects being the new oil pool discovery. Mort would carefully scrutinize Alberto's ideas and recommendations, and then act only on those that seemed to be the safest and surest. So many of these ideas worked, though, that even Mort eventually developed a feel for taking a chance, particularly after the initial risk had passed and a new idea was proven. Mort could not ride Alberto forever, however, and this became clear over the past year as Alberto began to openly chaff and fume under Mort's strict control. So when Mort was named a vice president and Alberto inquired about the general manager position in one of the other divisions, Mort decided to recommend Alberto for the job. Mort rarely let anyone on his staff transfer to another division without punishing them, but Alberto would be an exception, and it wouldn't hurt to have an ally elsewhere in the company.

So Alberto's ideas had provided Mort with a late career surge, one that made him a vice president. Still, Mort had squashed most of Alberto's riskier recommendations, and Mort now realized that squashing so many of these was probably one reason his division was now in trouble. Since Thanksgiving, though, Alberto had resurrected enough old ideas and combined them with enough new ones that Mort thought he had at least a fighting chance to revive his organization and perhaps get one more promotion—to president. But Mort would have to get lucky and have everything fall into place. And he realized that another tanker collision or new oil discovery weren't as statistically likely now as it had been for his former boss, who had skillfully used both to move on.

As he was thinking about all this, Mort spotted the sign for his exit from the interstate. He looked at his watch and then at the now-synchronized clock on his car's dashboard, and realized he would be home early. He began to plan the details of his evening. First, he would spend an hour going through the mail in the basket on the kitchen counter. Then, he would probably call Jen—she had not picked up when he called that morning and it had been a week since they last spoke. Finally, he would watch the local news before sitting down with a bottle of brandy in his leather chair to listen to Christmas music. Mort was not a big drinker, and three or four shots of brandy along with the music would make a nice tonic before bed.

Mort exited the interstate half a mile from home. He crept along on the side streets, purposely driving slow so he could enjoy the holiday decorations and lights on the exterior of the houses. As he approached his own house, he stopped the car in front of the adjacent home. There were no decorations on his own home, but he liked to look at his house from a distance. This was their twelfth house. They had moved all over the country in his thirty-two years with the company, and he liked this place the best. It was a two-story colonial with a brick facing. It was large— larger than they needed—and he had uncharacteristically overpaid for it. But it was an imposing house, particularly with the white columns. Jen hadn't been happy with the house, knowing she would have to clean it, but Mort finally agreed to hire a housekeeper. And then, to Mort's surprise, Jen turned her attention to the white columns.

Mort claimed the white columns were a highlight of the house, but Jen had studied architecture in college. She also worked three years for a design firm prior to marrying Mort, and she knew the columns were too large for the structure. The house was in a new subdivision and recently built, and it seemed to Jen that the columns had been tacked onto the otherwise plain, nondescript structure as an afterthought—perhaps to give it curb appeal so it would sell. For some reason, Jen was so sure of this that the columns became one of the few topics on which she refused to agree with Mort. So every time Mort made a favorable comment about the columns, eight years of architecture rose up in Jen and she commented negatively. That was the start of the rebellion.

With the children gone and a housekeeper now to keep the house clean, Jen began to get out. She made friends in the neighborhood, joined the local health club, and stopped taking drugs. Then Becky stopped eating and dropped thirty-five pounds in two months. When Becky passed out at work one day, Jen was summoned to a hospital in New Orleans. Mort was busy and couldn't travel, but managed to arrive three weeks later. Becky had been discharged to a clinic when Mort met up with her and Jen. After an initial interview, the clinic people said Mort could leave. This he was happy to do, because the interview had not gone well and he lost his temper. Mort visited Becky and Jen one additional time before Thanksgiving, but he then became busy with his recent promotion. Jen and Becky had been together now for four months.

So Mort sat in his car in front of his neighbor's house, admiring the white columns attached to the front of his brick-faced, colonial-style home. It was dark but the columns seemed to glow in the soft light thrown off by the street lamps, and there was even a splash of bright color reflected from one of the neighbors' outdoor Christmas lights. Creeping ahead now to his driveway, he was startled to observe a car parked on the concrete up near the garage. The car had been blocked from view by the house. He pulled up to it and glanced inside. He noticed a uniform jacket on the front seat. It looked like Larry had come.

Mort reached inside the glove box for the remote, pushed the button, and the garage door opened. He pulled his car into the garage and closed the door behind him. He got out of his car and made noise in the garage, even knocking over a stack of empty boxes, before rattling his keys for more than a minute as he finally opened the door to the kitchen. He coughed coming in the door, but detected a sudden run of feet across the living room followed by the sound of these same feet climbing stairs to the second floor. The basket of mail on the kitchen counter had been pushed to one side and some of the mail had been opened. He called out, "Larry? Is that you?"

There was no answer.

Then, again, "Larry? Are you here?"

"In here," came the reply. "Sorry, the volume was turned up." Larry was on his stomach, partially covered by blankets on the living room floor, lying between Mort's leather chair and the television set. Near him on the far side was the table on which the nativity scene was displayed.

"I didn't know you were coming," Mort said.

"My plans changed. I stopped in to see Mom and Becky, but that got old after a couple days and I drove back over to Fort Benning. That didn't work out either, and so I decided to come here—Mom gave me her key."

"When are you due back at the base?"

"Day after tomorrow."

"When do you ship out again?"

"Not until April."

"Well, Merry Christmas, Larry. It's good to see you."

"I'm sure it is. Merry Christmas to you, too, Dad."

"Did you come by yourself?"

"My friend is upstairs—said she wanted to get a shower. Her name is Yolanda. She doesn't speak English very well but she's no trouble—illegal, you know, if you get my drift."

"Yes, I suppose I do."

All this time, Larry stared directly at the television set. He was watching a video and Mort glanced at the set twice, turning away quickly each time.

"Hey, you should check this out—some old guy like yourself with young girls."

"No, Larry, I have no interest in that sort of thing."

"Maybe you should. An old toad like Mom can't be that exciting."

"OK, Larry, that's enough. Speaking of your mother, how is she?"

"She's actually lost some weight—she looks better. She's a better-looking old toad right now."

"Larry, that's enough."

"She's off the drugs—I couldn't sneak any from her like I used to. She also says she's feeling better—and thinking better. I don't know if she will put up with your crap the way she used to."

"Larry, that's enough."

"You keep bringing her up."

"Well, I won't anymore."

"Say, what's with Becky? She stopped eating and lost a bunch of weight—what the hell is that all about?"

"I'm not sure—some mumbo-jumbo about poor self-image. I don't get that stuff—those psychologists put things in your head."

"Someone abused her," Larry commented casually.

"Who said that?"

"The psychiatrist."

"What psychiatrist?"

"Becky has a psychiatrist—she asked to interview me. She asked a lot of questions—I could have killed the bitch. I finally told her to go to hell. Then I left."

The conversation lulled. Larry continued to stare into the television, and Mort could hear the water running through the pipes to the shower upstairs. Then the water stopped.

"You didn't put up any Christmas decorations—except for the nativity," said Larry. "And you don't have much to eat around here," Larry continued.

"Well, I haven't been home much lately."

"Where's the Baby Jesus? You put out the nativity set, but there's no Jesus."

"I haven't gotten around to Jesus yet."

"No Jesus? It's Christmas, Pop. The little fellow should be here."

"I'm sorry, Larry. I haven't been home."

"You never were home much."

"I was making a living, Larry—putting food on the table for you, your mother, and your sister. And putting a roof over our heads."

"Oh, come on, Pop. That's a load. You keep saying that, but everything you ever did was about you and for you."

"I don't think so! You've got that wrong, Larry!"

"Suite yourself. But have you got anything to eat?"

Mort never cooked and had dismissed the housekeeper, spending the last four months getting takeout on his way home from work. No shops or restaurants would be open on Christmas night, and so he scurried back into the kitchen and began looking through the cabinets. He found two cans of tamales in the pantry and frozen hot dogs and rolls in the freezer. He started heating it all up on the stove.

"Larry, I've warmed up a few things on the stove and it's about ready," Mort soon called from the kitchen. Larry came in a minute later, having put on white briefs.

"Great. What are we having?"

"Hot dogs and tamales—your friend might like the tamales—also, I found some canned fruit."

"Terrific! A real holiday feast!"

"Come on, Larry, it's the best I can do."

"Where were you today, anyway?"

"Down at your mother's brother's house."

"You mean at Frank and Cat's?"

"Yes."

"I always liked them. They had all those kids and there was always something to do there. And you sure had the hots for Cat, didn't you?"

"What are you talking about?"

"Everyone noticed it—particularly Mom. You would have liked to have her, wouldn't you? She's no toad. I'd even take a twirl with her."

"Cut it out, Larry. Can't you think of anything other than women?"

"No. Just women and guns. And war. I like war. I get to shoot people without retribution. I get to decide who lives and dies."

"Cut it out, Larry. Where's your friend?"

"I don't think she's coming down. She said she wanted to rest after the shower. I've been keeping her busy, if you get what I mean."

They ate in silence on stools against the kitchen counter. Larry had turned off the television and it was quiet in the house. It occurred to Mort that they ate hot dogs the last time Larry was home, at their previous house when he brought two of his military buddies over on the Fourth of July. All three of them arrived half-drunk and stayed only two hours. Both of Larry's friends spoke highly of Larry, and it became apparent they looked up to him. The three kept to themselves most of the time, laughing and talking and clowning around. Finally, when they were all about to leave, one of Larry's friends came over to Mort and said, "Larry's a man—a real man! You should see him in action—a killing machine! He don't take no prisoners—a perfect killing machine!" Mort winced at the memory of it.

Finally, Mort said, "We ate hot dogs the last time you were home—remember that Fourth of July three years ago?"

"Yep. I came with Sam and Johnny. We had wieners and burgers and you even bought steak."

"Yes. Your buddies seemed like nice guys—where are they now?"

"Sam lost his legs near Mosul. I lost track of Johnny—he was half-crazy anyway."

"Lost his legs—what happened?"

"Roadside bomb. Last time I heard, he was up in Maryland getting new legs."

"Maybe you'll get to see him sometime."

"What for? I don't want to see him—he's a loser. Couldn't keep himself together."

"That's a hard thing to say."

"You have to take care of yourself—you have to take care of Number One. You taught me that. The hell with everyone else."

"I didn't teach you that."

"Sure you did. I got eighteen years of it. And I learned it well."

"I did not teach you that!"

"Oh yes you did!"

Just then, Yolanda appeared in the doorway from the living room. She was small and looked young—maybe eighteen, Mort hoped. Mort thought her face looked odd, but she was hanging back in the shadows and couldn't quite clearly be seen.

"Hey Babe!" said Larry.

Yolanda nodded.

"You want some tamales?"

She nodded yes.

"I'll be done in a minute—me and Pop were just having a serious father-son conversation."

"I don't think she understood that," Mort offered.

"Of course she didn't. I didn't pick her up for her brains. Here, finish this," and Larry handed her his plate. She came into the light and Mort gasped—her face was bruised and purple."

"What's wrong with you?" Larry asked.

"Her face—something is wrong with her face."

"No joke."

"You've got to see about it. I think she needs a doctor."

"I don't think so. She goes to the doctor and she gets deported. And maybe I get arrested—I don't think so. She's just a skank anyway."

Mort felt sick. He rose suddenly to his feet and lurched toward the sink, vomiting. Larry began to laugh. Then he couldn't stop laughing.

"What the hell is wrong with you!" Mort finally said, after running water in the sink and using a cup to rinse his mouth.

"Oh, come on, Pop."

"What's wrong with you!"

"Oh, come on. I did worse to Becky—it didn't even show with Becky!"

Mort paused for a moment. "You bastard! You sick, filthy bastard!" Mort exclaimed.

"Now, now, Pop. Get it all out. Get it all out, Pop, and you'll feel better."

"You need to go! You need to go—now! Get out or I'll call the police!"

"Come on, Pop. You're killing me, Pop—just killing me. You must like the drama."

"Get out or I'll call the police!"

"Tell you what. I can take a hint—I can tell when I'm not welcome. But I'm a little thin in the finance department. Why don't you make a small investment in my future—give me a few bucks—enough to get food and a motel room for me and my Latin queen for a couple of nights. You have plenty of money anyway—Mom said so. And your bank statements say so," and Larry gestured toward Mort's opened mail.

Mort cursed and went to his study, pulling five one-hundred dollar bills from a drawer of his desk. Then he returned to the kitchen—flinging the money at Larry.

"Now, that's a good fella. Thanks, Pop. This has been a wonderful Christmas after all. I'll say hello to Mom for you if I see her—I don't think she's planning to come back here anytime soon. In fact, I don't think she's coming back here at all. Have a very Merry Christmas, Pop!" And ten minutes later, Larry and the girl were gone.

Mort cleaned himself up in the bathroom off the front hallway. He rinsed this time with mouthwash and dusted the dried food splatter off the front of his shirt. Then he gathered up the blankets from the living room floor and piled them in the laundry room. He returned to his study and retrieved a bottle of brandy from the cabinet behind his desk. He fumbled with the cap, spilling about as much brandy as he was able to dump into a glass. He took a gulp. It burned as it went down, and he gagged. He waited a minute for the brandy to settle, and then took another gulp. Five minutes and five gulps later, he began to relax.

He returned to the kitchen with the brandy and his glass. He resolved to put the events with Larry behind him, so he could get on with his evening. He busied himself by wiping off the stove and counters, and by putting the plates and pots from dinner into the dishwasher. After fifteen minutes, the kitchen gleamed and shined. Then, he took the basket of mail and retreated to his study. He honed in quickly on the bank statements. These were statements for his joint account with Jen, and he had not looked at these for two months. Statements for his personal accounts came to the office, and he regularly reviewed them there. He was surprised to find the balance on the joint account at nearly zero. Jen had recently asked him to put more money into the account, so she could make withdrawals to help Becky, and he had put in another ten thousand just two weeks before. The most recent statement indicated twenty thousand had been taken out in the last month alone.

And now, suddenly, he felt very tired and woozy. He would have taken a shower and turned in for the night, except that it was Christmas, and so he went to the darkened living room. He flipped the switch to activate the nativity set lights, bathing the display in a bright glow. He used the remote to turn on the stereo and, as the music began, he sank into his leather chair with his brandy. The shepherds and wise men gazed serenely from the nearby table, and all seemed calm and all seemed bright. It occurred to him that he should go and retrieve Jesus out of the nativity set box in the closet, but he procrastinated. He also forgot to call Jen. Soon, he was asleep in his chair. The music finished ten minutes later.

# The Parts Business

It was that same dream. He was fifteen-years-old and standing in the mud of his grandfather's salvage yard. He had just sold an engine out of a '52 Pontiac for $90, after getting $65 for a fender off a '59 Impala. The Pontiac had a hood ornament with an Indian that lighted up, and the same guy who bought the engine gave him $70 for both the Indian hood ornament and the hood it was mounted on. His grandfather then drove up in the wrecker with a '64 Ford Fairlane hanging off the back.

"Here's $225, Grandpa. I sold a fender and hood and also a motor while you were gone."

"Where's your uncle?" asked Grandpa.

"Inside."

"Did he help you?"

"No. He said he was busy."

"Useless fool," grandfather said. "Here, you keep $25—I want you to have it. You've got a nose for the salvage business. I'm glad you're here. You do a hell of a job."

"Thanks, Grandpa."

"I mean it, boy. You're the best I've got—that includes your two uncles and your cousins."

And that was always the end of the dream. The dream was a replay of an actual incident, one that occurred almost forty years earlier. This particular incident was the first in a sequence of related events, but he always woke up before the rest of the events played out. The dream always ended where it ended because the rest of the sequence included the death of his grandfather two months later; then the ugly feud over his grandfather's property; and finally his being put out on his own three months after that. He first had the dream fifteen years ago, and then once or twice a year thereafter. The dream was a consolation to him, and he always woke up afterwards feeling better. If he had believed in God, he might even have claimed it was heaven-sent.

Sitting up in bed, he checked the clock on the night stand. It was almost six, and so he got up and shaved and dressed. Then he went downstairs to the bar for breakfast. It was a bright, brilliant morning and the sun streamed in from the large, wide window that opened out over the bay. A girl came out from behind the bar and took his order as dolphins suddenly appeared on the waters of the bay.

"Are those sharks?" he blurted, to no one in particular.

"Dolphins," said someone from two tables away.

"You're sure? They look like sharks."

"They're dolphins—like those on the wall."

On the wall behind the bar, just to the right of the large window, was a wide mural with a group of three dolphins swimming in the waters of the bay. The near dolphin was submerged with only its dorsal fin exposed, but the mural captured the rounded heads and noses of two other dolphins as they surfaced from the water. Just then, the rounded noses of several live dolphins became visible outside as they looped in and out of the waters of the bay.

"Sharks don't have rounded noses, do they?"

"No."

"That painting on the wall—it's almost exactly like the scene outside—it's amazing."

"Yes, it is."

The girl came over and poured more coffee. There were just the two of them at the bar that morning, each having breakfast at a separate table facing the large window and bay outside. Because the mural of the dolphins was adjacent to the large window, one could easily shift gaze back and forth from the mural to the bay.

"Sorry to have bothered you, I should have introduced myself—I'm Jack O'Dell," called the first man.

"It's not a bother—I'm Clint Farrier," replied the second man from two tables away.

"You must know something about dolphins."

"Not really, but I'm a regular here and I've gotten the same answer to the same question you just asked about the dolphins."

"You come here often?"

"Every two weeks. I'm in the medical equipment and supply business."

"I was in that business for four years. I sold prostheses—legs and arms and such. It was a good business at first; then just about everyone started selling arms and legs and the margin went to almost nothing. I couldn't make any money at it."

"What do you do now?"

"I'm between jobs. I had an accident—hurt my back and leg. Except for a good surgeon, I might be limping around on one of those fake legs I used to sell."

"I'm sorry to hear that. I hope your recovery is going well."

"Another couple of months and I can work again, if I want."

"So what will you do this time?"

"Sell something—I've always been in sales. Started out selling car parts; then sold farm equipment and tractor parts; finally ended up selling the whole tractor for a while. Next came Chryslers and after that, the four years selling prostheses. I even sold computers and computer parts when they first came out. I made some real money then—but you have to get in early. The real money is early on when a product just catches on but before everyone else gets into it. The last thing was mutual funds—actually derivatives—but I prefer selling something I can see—cars or computers or parts of things like cars or computers. I'm old fashioned that way. There's money to be made in sales if you get the right situation."

"What brings you here?"

"I'm down to see one of my daughters—she's a nurse interning at one of the hospitals—first time I've been here."

"It's a nice town. Not too big, but big enough to have three hospitals and plenty of doctors and some clinics. It's slow and quiet for a coastal town and out of the mainstream."

"It seems like a nice place."

"Well, I've got to go," said the dolphin expert, rising to leave. "Nice to meet you, Jack. Maybe we'll run into each other again."

"Maybe so. Good luck today with your medical equipment."

The dolphin expert nodded and left.

Jack sat at his table a few minutes longer. He retrieved a small plastic bottle from the inside of his jacket and opened it, removing a pill. He took the pill with half a glass of water. The pill was for pain and he had been working steadily to wean himself off the medication. He was down to two pills a day—the first in the morning and then a second in the evening so he could sleep. Over the past two months, he had cut his intake from six pills a day to now just two, and he felt good about it. He couldn't drink alcohol as long as he was taking the pills, and he hoped to be drinking again soon.

Late that morning, he went to meet his daughter for lunch. He arrived early and bought a newspaper while he waited, but he was too nervous to read it. It was awkward when they first met, and he noticed he was more nervous than even she was. He hadn't seen her in eight years, and she had turned out a beautiful girl. He noticed right off that her mouth and the set of her jaw was just like his, and he didn't recall the resemblance being so strong. It was the same mouth and jaw of his second daughter, Lucy, who he last saw three years earlier.

"I'm sorry, but I couldn't help but notice your limp—is your leg bothering you?" she asked as they sat down for lunch.

"I was in a car accident. It was a nasty wreck and I hurt my back and leg. I was one of the lucky ones, though, two others died and a third was mangled pretty bad. I got out of it with some cracked vertebrae and a leg put back together with screws and a plate. I have a settlement coming and should be able to help more with school."

"You've helped enough. You've paid for nearly all of it."

"Still, I want to help where I can. I'm sorry I haven't seen you much."

"Mom didn't want you around. I always liked it when you visited, but Mom didn't. I know you tried to see me and always remembered my birthday and holidays, so I'm grateful for that. But I'm older now and I can see whom I want. I wanted to see you again."

"How is school going for you?"

"I'll be finished this semester. I like nursing and it has gone well for me."

"What then? Have you thought about specializing?"

"Not right now. I want to get some experience. I might even try to work overseas with an aid organization or for a charity. I want to work with poor people and with children. You might remember that I went on a mission for a year after high school—you sent money for it. That was a good experience."

"I remember. There are plenty of poor people here in the states, though, and children."

"I know. I've been volunteering at a counseling center for women—mostly unwed mothers who are expecting. They also have a shelter and clinic. It's through church. I might stay here—I haven't ruled out anything yet."

"Well, you still have time to figure it all out. Things should be wide open for you—the medical field is booming and they need nurses everywhere. You can make some serious money for someone just starting out."

The meeting with his daughter was successful, and they met again for supper that evening. They then agreed to meet in a couple of weeks. This was his first daughter, Emily, who he had with his second wife. His second wife had been a stiff and religious woman, and the marriage lasted only six years. He had a second daughter from his third wife, and he had not seen his second daughter in three years. His third wife had been a rabbit of sorts—jumping in and out of different beds with different men, and finally she had jumped for good and taken their daughter, Lucy, with her. He made monthly payments to his third wife for fourteen years, and so was able to keep track of his second daughter this way, but two years ago Lucy turned eighteen and he lost contact. Lucy and her mother had moved around a lot, but their last address was a town less than fifty miles from Emily. He wondered if somehow Lucy and Emily had met, and he had asked Emily about it, but Emily said no. He had even stopped at the last address he had for Lucy on his drive down to see Emily, but there were new people at the address.

Jack had been thinking more than usual since his accident, not being able to work and having more free time than he was accustomed to. This thinking had led him to the realization that he had loved only one of his wives—the first. It took two additional wives and more than fifteen years of fasting from wives to recognize this, but he was sure of it now. This first wife had been a shy and generous woman from a large and close family whom he met at school when he lived with his grandfather. They married shortly after she finished high school, while he was working at another salvage yard. They were together four years before Jack was offered a job selling tractor parts in another town. This job went so well that Jack was offered a job selling whole tractors two counties away, and he accepted it on the spot, only to find out his wife didn't want to go with him. Jack felt like he had to take the job selling tractors, and so they entered into an arrangement where Jack would get home on the weekends. Jack enjoyed selling things—anything—and he was a natural at it. After four years selling tractors, Jack took a job selling Chryslers on the other side of the state. A month later, after they had been married for nine years, Jack's first wife filed for divorce. Of all the things he regretted in his life, he regretted this first failed marriage the most and also that he and his first wife had been unable to conceive a child.

Jack's second wife was a devout woman who sang in a Baptist choir. Jack felt guilty after his first divorce and thought he needed straightening-up, so he hooked up with the Baptist wife soon after. This second wife forbade him to drink and cuss, though they both smoked, and she generally policed him fairly rigorously. She didn't mind the long hours he spent at work because of the money it brought in, and soon Jack was working longer hours than ever. He would leave the house in the morning at eight, sell cars from nine in the morning to nine at night, spend an hour in the bar, then drive home and be in bed by eleven. This he did six days a week but, on the seventh, he went to church with his second wife. This worked flawlessly for six years. Then one spring, after he and the second wife watched a replay on television of the second wife and her Baptist choir's Easter performance, there followed another short replay segment—this time of the local Mardi Gras parade. Sure enough, Jack could be seen waving drunkenly from a float belonging to one of the local car dealerships. There was then a short, shrill confrontation and Jack spent the following two nights on the couch. On the third day, Jack was served divorce papers.

Like the second wife, Jack's third wife was a rebound from the immediately preceding wife. This third wife, Lana, was a devious and libidinous woman who liked to spread her libidinousness around. Jack was just happy to have someone warm and friendly to lie up against at night, and Lana was happy to have Jack go off and work all day so she could get warm and friendly with someone else. This marriage lasted five years. Then, he came home one evening to find the house cleaned out. A month later, he began paying child support.

Two weeks after his first visit with Emily, Jack was back eating breakfast at the motel with the dolphin mural in the bar. He spent most of that afternoon with Emily, and then returned to the motel and sat in the bar. The bar was busy at night and a popular gathering place. He had ginger ale and a pain pill. He wished he could get off the pills and begin drinking again. He then ran into the dolphin expert as he passed a conference room on the way to his room, calling out, "Hello, Clint! Jack O'Dell here—remember? It's a small world, isn't it? Nice to see you again!"

Clint recognized him and they shook hands. "Back to see your daughter?"

"Yes, as a matter of fact. Medical supply business doing okay?"

"Yes, but very busy. I've been on the run lately."

"What's going on here?" Jack inquired, nodding toward the conference room.

"The monthly meeting of the local conservation society—Bay City Conservation Alliance. They meet to discuss issues like sewage discharge, beach erosion, plastic in the water, and saving sea turtles and baby dolphins and the like. It turns out the bay and estuary here are a giant nursery for all kinds of marine life. I stop in sometimes to hear what they have to say, and maybe put twenty dollars in their jar afterwards, and they are always appreciative. I'm just trying to do my part to keep the bay here clean and natural."

"Being a good corporate citizen—that's good business, Clint."

"Absolutely."

"Will they let you advertise? Can you mention your business and such?"

"Oh no, it's not that kind of situation. And besides, I prefer to work behind the scenes. I would never advertise."

"Oh, right."

Just then, Clint's cell phone rang and he waved and withdrew down the hallway. As this call ended, there was a second call and then a third. Jack waited around for fifteen minutes, but then went to his room.

Clint was on the phone again the next morning when Jack found him in the bar at breakfast. "The medical supply business must be good," Jack commented when Clint finally got off the phone.

"Yes, too good, sometimes. I'm having trouble being in two places at once."

"I've known that feeling. You have to jump when business is good because it can be mighty slow other times. You have to make hay while the sun shines."

"Yes, you do."

Clint's phone rang again. Jack got up to leave and went to get something out of his room before going out for the day. Jack was stopped at the front desk twenty minutes later when he saw Clint again.

"Checking out?" Clint inquired.

"Oh no, I've got another day here."

"Plans with your daughter?"

"I do this evening. This morning I'm going to just drive around a bit—see the area a little more."

"Say, Jack, let's talk a minute," and Clint guided him off to the side. "Look, Jack, I'm as busy as I could be right now. I need some temporary help and if you are interested, I might be able to use you. Nothing physically demanding—just pick up and deliver some packages. I've got a package to be picked up and put on a plane this morning, and I'll pay you well to do it."

"Oh, you don't have to pay, Clint. I'd be happy to help out. Just tell me where and when to pick up the package. No big deal."

"I can't let you do it for nothing. I insist on paying. Who knows, if you don't mind doing this, there may be more work of this type. It's not strenuous and won't wear you out. But it is the type of work that has to be handled just right."

"Pay me if you want. Just give me some instructions and I'll take care of it."

Two hours later, Jack was waiting in the lobby of another motel. A thin young man with a package under his arm appeared abruptly before him. He was sweating and seemed to be in a hurry.

"Are you Jack O'Dell?"

"One and the same."

"I'm Jeremy. I was told to bring this to you. Here's an address for a freight service at the airport. The package should be there before eleven—you have about half an hour to get it there."

"No problem. Oh my, it's cold!"

"Packed in ice. It's in a special carton so it will keep. Get it to the airport as soon as you can."

"What is it?"

Jeremy paused. Then he laughed and said, "Seafood."

"Okay, I'm on my way."

Jack made the delivery. Afterwards, he was able to get out and drive around, and then he met his daughter for supper in the evening. He was back at the motel by nine o'clock, finding Clint in the bar. Clint gave him one hundred dollars, cash.

"Oh, that's too much—way too much."

"You earned every penny as far as I'm concerned. I'm more than happy to give it to you."

"This is too easy—like stealing. A hundred dollars to deliver a package of seafood?"

"Seafood? Who said it was seafood?"

"Jeremy."

"Oh, Jeremy—he likes to joke around. You didn't deliver seafood—those were organs—a liver, a thymus, and a kidney."

"Organs? You mean human organs? Parts?"

"Not parts—call them organs. Or specialized tissues. As you know, I'm in the medical supply business. Part of my businesses is to provide organs and tissue from various donors to hospitals and universities—for transplants and research and such. That's why the packages are kept cold—they have to be delivered quickly and on time."

"Well, it's easy work, like you said."

"But it has to be done right. I have another package for tomorrow. Do you want to stay over and make the delivery? Same money as today and I'll even cover your motel room."

"Sure," Jack replied casually. "Just tell me where and when."

Jack actually delivered two packages the next day, and then stayed over one more night and delivered another. He picked up the two packages at the same motel lobby he picked up his first package, but the last package was exchanged on the side of the road where Jeremy's car broke down. Jeremy rode with Jack to the airport and waited in the car. Then Jack dropped Jeremy off at a white, cinder block building on the opposite side of town near the harbor, next to a coin-operated laundry. The cinder block building had a sign reading, "Biomedical Supply, Inc."

Ten days later, Clint and Jack met again for breakfast in the bar with the dolphins. They had talked twice by phone since their last meeting, and Jack was set to deliver four packages over the next two days. These would be the last deliveries he would make. He felt uneasy taking so much money for such simple work, and he had told this to Clint. He delivered the first two packages that morning, and then went to meet his daughter for lunch early that afternoon. She was late, so he bought a paper and began scanning the front page. There, at the bottom, was a photo of a beached dolphin. The belly of the dolphin was cut open and a man pointed inside. The caption said the dolphin died from ingesting plastic caps and bottles.

"Oh my. Did you see this?" Jack remarked to Emily when they met.

"Oh, the dolphin story," Emily replied.

"Yes, the plastic in the bay must be pretty bad. They found bottles and caps in the fish's stomach."

"Dolphins aren't fish, Dad. Their mammals—like us."

"Oh, I didn't know that. I never took much science in school."

"They found more than just plastic in that dolphin. They found part of a baby's leg and a hand. They came to the hospital about it, but we couldn't do anything."

"How did a baby's hand and leg end up in a dolphin?"

"Sometimes medical waste gets dumped in the bay. Not from us, but from one or two of the clinics."

"How do babies end up in medical waste?"

"It's called abortion, Dad. That was probably part of an aborted baby."

"Oh Lord!" He was shocked and sat stunned for a moment. Then he wasn't hungry. When his daughter said she had a late breakfast, they went outside to walk the concrete path along the bay.

"Your limp seems to be getting a little better," his daughter said.

"Yes, I think so. Thanks for noticing."

"Are you still in pain?"

"Yes, a little. I'm still taking pain pills, but I can't get completely off them yet. I'm down to one pill a day—at night to sleep."

"Well, you're making progress. That stuff you are taking isn't supposed to be addictive, but you never know. Keep weaning yourself off of it if you can."

"I will. I'm trying." He wanted to drink badly.

The following morning he was in the lobby of the motel where he normally met Jeremy. His phone rang.

"This is Jeremy. I'm really busy. Just come here and pick up the package—I can't bring it to you right now and the package has to be delivered on time."

"I'm coming now. I'll meet you where I dropped you off last time."

"No, not there—next door. Just wait in the laundromat. I'll bring the package to you."

"The laundromat?"

"Yes. Just be there. Meet me at the laundromat."

Jack was at the laundry in fifteen minutes. He waited in his car, but finally got out and went inside. There were only two people, an old black man and a fat, middle-aged white woman, both waiting for their clothes to dry. He lingered inside for ten minutes or so, but then went outside and walked around to the back of the building. The white, cinder block building where he had dropped off Jeremy previously was just across a narrow parking lot. He decided to go over and find Jeremy. Rounding the front of the building, he made for the entrance. The door was locked and the place appeared to be deserted, but he noticed cars and some foot traffic at the adjacent building farther down. He started for this other building but suddenly pulled up. For a moment, he thought he recognized someone entering this other building, but then Jeremy's voice called from behind.

"Hey—over here. I thought I told you to wait at the laundromat."

"I waited. You never came. I've been looking for you."

"Well, I'm right here. Come inside. The package isn't quite ready or I would have been over. You don't want to be wandering around out here. Someone will call the police."

"Call the police—what for?"

"There's always trouble. Protesters, do-gooders, holy-rollers. We've had to get an injunction to keep them away. They still try sometimes, though. Come on in and sit down. I'm almost done and you'll be out of here in a few minutes."

Jack stared blankly at Jeremy, not quite comprehending.

"You don't understand any of this, do you?" said Jeremy. "You must be one of the densest people I've ever met."

"What are you talking about?"

"That's a women's clinic next door."

"A what?"

"A women's clinic—an abortion clinic. Come on—wise up. And this," Jeremy gestured around him, "is the place where we take babies to prepare them for distribution."

"Distribution?"

"We harvest the parts."

"Oh, Lord, I had no idea."

"You're a little slow on the uptake. The packages you deliver are human body parts—going to labs and hospitals across the country. The babies are brought here, to this building, and I part them out in the back room. I might have flunked out of medical school, but I know where everything is—as long as the baby isn't dismembered too badly. But they're getting better next door with the extraction. They're providing some decent product and there's good money in this when it all goes right."

Jack sank into a chair. His mind was whirling and he was trying to think. Jeremy left the room and, for several minutes, Jack just sat and thought. Finally, Jeremy reentered the room with the package. Then Jack spoke up, "Have you ever seen them do it."

"Do what?"

"Abort a baby."

"Of course. Many times. Depending on what the client wants, I sometimes have to be there right as the baby comes out—it all depends. Some clients want the product as fresh as possible, others don't care too much about the condition—they're just looking for a certain type of tissue. Sometimes they want whole, intact organs. I've even boxed-up live babies for shipment—sedated, of course. Oh, wait—I forgot the shipping label—I'll be back in a minute."

Jack slumped back into his chair. He waited. He was thinking about the person he thought he had recognized earlier. When Jeremy came back into the room again with the package, Jack stood up and said, "I want to see what goes on over there."

"Oh, sure—just like that! Are you crazy?"

"No, just curious."

"Or sick, maybe."

"Okay, sick." And Jack winked and grinned.

"You're a sick one, all right. Tell you what. The nurse next door just called and I've got to go over there. I'll take you with me, but you have to do exactly as I say. This can be a touchy business."

"Of course."

Jack followed Jeremy out of the room. Jeremy stopped for a moment to put the package in a refrigerator in the adjacent room, and then they both entered a short hallway that ended at a closed door. Jack figured the closed door connected the cinder block building to the clinic, and this was confirmed when they opened it and passed through. A nurse was standing at a desk about fifty feet down the hallway into the clinic.

"Sign these papers," said the nurse. "Who's he?"

"The courier. Just wants to have a look."

"You shouldn't have brought him here. This isn't the circus."

"Or not the usual kind," Jeremy quipped. "We'll just be a few minutes. He wants to see the action."

"You're sick."

"Not me—him. And he's already admitted that."

"Well, you're out of luck. We had that one last girl scheduled, but she lost her nerve. She just bolted out of here—a wreck."

"You couldn't give her some drugs?"

"We gave her drugs, but she was a mess when she came in. Angry as hell at that creep boyfriend she came with—the father, I think. She started thrashing around and we couldn't restrain her, and I'm not comfortable proceeding with someone in that condition."

"Where's doc? Why didn't he do it?"

"Had a golf game. It's been a tough day. We've been running late from the moment I got here this morning. Doc took off a half hour ago."

"Well, that's too bad. My friend here will be disappointed." And Jeremy nodded toward Jack, who was reading a chart on the nurse's desk. Jack made out the first name, but didn't recognize the second. He made a mental note of the address.

"You need to go, Jeremy. Sign this paper and then take your friend with you."

"In a minute. Let me just show him something first." Jeremy took Jack into a small observation space adjacent to a room with a table. "Well, here is where it all happens—this room and another like it. On a good day, we get ten or eleven women. That's almost a full delivery room there—like in a hospital. Just bring in the girls, strap 'em down, get their feet in the stirrups, and away we go."

"Amazing."

A minute later, they were back in the hallway. The nurse was seated at the desk, and as Jeremy turned to leave, she said to him, "I'll call you tomorrow morning. That girl might have gotten away again, but those drugs we gave her will put her into labor. Then she'll be back. Tell Clint it will cost him extra for a live fetus. Doc said she was seven months the last time that creep brought her in, but Doc isn't always right about things like that. Just be sure you're available when the baby comes out."

Then Jack and Jeremy left. Back in the cinder block building, Jeremy said, "Look, Jack, I have no more work here today. I'll take the package to the airport myself—I could use the money."

Jack nodded and walked back to the laundry and his car next door.

That night, Jack looked for Clint at the bar with the dolphins. Clint was sipping his drink at the counter when Jack sat down beside him and said, "Hello, Clint. I had the opportunity today to pay a visit to that place where Jeremy works. The two of you have an interesting business."

"Now, Jack, it's not what you think…"

"Here's what I think and I've been thinking about this all afternoon. I'll admit that I was offended at first, but then I tried to look on the positive side and realized this could be a great public service to those with debilitating illness—Parkinson's or Alzheimer's or whatever. A business to harvest organs and tissue can be a great help to the sick. It can be almost a heroic sort of activity."

Clint looked at Jack carefully, wondering if he was being put on.

"And, you know, Clint, I wouldn't mind being involved in this with you, but I think I should be getting a bigger cut of the pie."

"Well, Jack, tell you what. I'll cut you in—I'm just swamped. The live births are a real problem for me—they require particular care and I'm again supposed to be in two places at the same time tomorrow morning. Let's see what we can work out. There's enough money here for the two of us."

The next morning, Jack was at the laundromat at eight. By eight-fifteen, he had walked over to the cinder block building and Jeremy had let him inside. An hour and a half later, a baby girl was delivered in the adjacent clinic. The baby was still-born, and Jeremy took it away. "She was tiny," the nurse had commented to Jeremy. "I don't think she was even six months. The Doc just isn't real good estimating gestation. He should probably drink less and golf more and try to get himself in better shape. We'll try for another live one this afternoon. That girl from yesterday should be back."

"I'll put this one on ice until I hear something from Clint," Jeremy had responded. "He called this morning and said the courier will handle all live births from now on, but I think he still wants to handle ones like this himself."

At two that afternoon, Jeremy came down the hallway and through the door to the cinder block building with a baby boy wrapped in a towel. The boy was quiet and seemed lethargic, and Jeremy said the baby got some of the sedation given to his mother. This would make him easier to ship, Jeremy assured Jack, as he placed the boy carefully in an insulated shipping carton. Then Jack paid Jeremy, took the carton, and walked quickly to the laundry next door. Emily was waiting in the car, and Jack handed her the carton just as the child began to wail. Emily opened the box in the back seat, removed the boy from the towel, and wrapped him in a blanket. She had a bottle ready and lay down on the seat with the baby, as Jack drove out of the laundry parking lot and started down the street past the cinder block building. Passing the clinic, Jack saw a nurse leading Lucy out the front door. Lucy was stumbling and crying, hysterical and barely able to walk. The boyfriend followed behind, casually lighting a cigarette. Jack set his jaw and steered straight ahead.

That was the start. Over the next eleven weeks, Jack bought nineteen babies—every live birth the clinic had. Ten of the babies survived—six white ones, three black ones, and one brown one. Jack and Emily brought all nineteen to the shelter and clinic where Emily was a volunteer, and no questions were asked. Of the nine babies that did not survive, four were so premature that they died in his car on the way to the shelter. Three more were nearly stillborn—exiting the mother alive but succumbing before Jeremy could even walk them down the hallway to the cinder block building. Two more were born with gross defects and expired quickly—one with arms like flippers, and the other a black boy with a head shaped like an eggplant and no eyes—just vague openings sealed shut. The black boy made a strange gurgling noise as he gasped for air, but he was a fighter and lasted more than half an hour. Though Jack usually drove so Emily could care for the babies on their way to the clinic, this wasn't the case with the black boy who had no eyes—Jack made Emily drive so he could cradle the child in his arms, crying for the boy as Emily drove along. Jack cried for the boy with the eggplant head, cried for himself, and cried for all the other orphans who had no one to love them, no one who wanted them, and no place to lay their heads.

After he bought his nineteenth baby, Jack ran out of money. At about this same time, the doctor at the clinic where Jeremy worked started to drink less and play more golf, until he no longer felt comfortable delivering live fetuses. By this time, Clint was completely out of the baby business and no longer procuring parts, and Jeremy got laid off. For three weeks, Jack didn't know what to do, but then the settlement from his car accident came in and Jack was back in business. Jack had big money now, could compete aggressively for the product, and bought four new babies in the next two weeks from a clinic up the coast. Jack also realized that he would never be able to quite corner the entire market, but resolved to participate where he could. Though he was no longer an energetic young man selling car or computer parts, this was one business where he was certain it was better to deal in the whole commodity. He felt good about the baby business and it had evolved into a sort of family enterprise—his daughter Emily had lined up funding and sponsors through church to purchase even more babies. He thought he might even be able to franchise the business—there were three nuns backed by a charity interested in expanding his operation to the other side of the state.

One night late that year, just before Christmas, Jack had that dream again. He was with his grandfather in the mud of the salvage yard, after his grandfather had arrived in the wrecker with the '64 Fairlane hanging off the back. His grandfather had just given him the $25 and told him he was a hell of a worker—the best he had. Normally, he would have awakened at this point, but the dream played on a little longer—jumping to a scene two months later. This scene was of a crane lifting a truck in the salvage yard and, suddenly, the sound of a loud snap and a cable whipping about. Then he saw his grandfather face-down in the mud, half-severed above the waist. He screamed and ran to his grandfather, who jerked his head sideways and spoke these last, few, words, "Tell grandma I love her. You—you're like a son—the best!" And then his grandfather was gone. And finally, for the first time in his life, Jack knew that someone had loved him and he woke up.

Sitting up in bed, Jack realized he hadn't been able to completely recall this last incident in the salvage yard before. He felt suddenly light, and he turned on the lamp and got out of bed. He sat in a nearby chair and looked for the clock—it was half past three. He was in his own house on the coast overlooking the bay—a condominium he recently purchased after selling his place up north. His two daughters and grandson were nearby, in another condominium down the street. He suddenly felt a sharp pain in his back and went to the bathroom to get water for another pill. He was back up to four pills a day, because he hurt his back again when he went to get Lucy.

Jack found Lucy in a dilapidated house, motorcycle parts strewn about on the porch. The house sat in a yard filled with car bodies on cinder blocks, patrolled by three dogs, all inside a chain link fence. Jack took care of the dogs with tainted meat, but the boyfriend required a different approach. The boyfriend had a knife and wanted to use it, but Jack was in familiar territory and knew something about junkyard fights. Jack lunged awkwardly to avoid the knife, wrenching his back, but still swung deftly with a tire iron and caught the boyfriend hard over the left ear. At first, Jack thought the tire iron might have killed him, but the boyfriend emerged from a coma after three days with only a skull fracture and permanent hearing loss in the one ear. The boyfriend got ten years for attempted murder, seven more for aggravated assault on an outstanding warrant, and then another five years for armed burglary on an additional warrant. Lucy, with tears of joy and relief, got to leave the dilapidated house.

Jack swallowed his pill in the bathroom and returned to the chair by his bed. As he sat there waiting for his medication to kick in, it occurred to him that he might never be able to drink again. After a while, he shut off the light and peered out the window and across the moonlit waters of the bay. The moon was full and the visibility better than he expected. He was looking for dolphins.

# Mother Goes To Mars

Mother was born in Chicago in 1921. Her parents were Henry and Josephine, and she had an older brother named Joseph, who was born in 1918. Mother was said to be a lively child who collected dolls and enjoyed playing outdoors. Joseph was a frail child with asthma.

Henry, Mother's father, knew something about electrons and how to move them properly through switches and wires. Henry became a successful electrical construction engineer and even ran his own electrical contracting business during the Depression. Henry spent his last twenty years running operations for another electrical contractor, and he was a good provider for his family.

Because Henry was a good provider, Mother and her family took trips. There was a trip to New York in 1925 and a second trip to Florida and Cuba in 1928. On the trip to Florida and Cuba, the asthma left Joseph. It must have hung around, though, because it was looking for Mother in 1929 after she had a bout of the whooping cough. The asthma found Mother, crawled into her lungs, and stayed there.

Mother began to be absent from school because of asthma in the fifth grade. Joseph had burned a green powder, called Asthmador, in a tin when he had the asthma and inhaling the fumes had brought relief. Mother began to burn the Asthmador, but it didn't always bring relief. Soon, a spray of adrenalin chloride was prescribed and, for the next ten or fifteen years, this spray was Mother's primary medication. In the most severe asthma attacks, Mother was injected with morphine.

At the end of the fifth grade, there began a crusade to drive the asthma out of Mother. The doctors first tested Mother for allergies, and though there was some reaction to milk and feathers, eliminating exposure to them brought little relief. Then Josephine took Mother on another trip to Florida, in the hope the asthma would leap out of Mother the same way it had leapt out of Joseph three years earlier. But asthma found the moist, balmy, Florida air to be congenial, and on this second Florida trip the asthma actually worsened. They next tried to coax the asthma out of Mother in North Carolina, taking a cottage in the Smokies for three months after the doctors suggested a mountain climate might drive the asthma out. It didn't, and Mother returned to Chicago and began high school.

Mother entered Trinity High School in Chicago in 1935. This was a Dominican school for girls and a companion to Fenwick, a Dominican school for boys, attended by Joseph. In high school, Mother showed an interest in sketching and art and developed a talent in this area. In 1939, Mother graduated high school and entered Rosary College for women, a school two blocks from the high school and run by the same order of Dominican nuns. Mother was unable to finish the first term at Rosary College because of her asthma. This time, the doctors recommended a desert climate for Mother. So Josephine and Mother rented another cottage, this time in Arizona, and for the first time since she was eight, Mother could breathe somewhat normally.

In the fall of 1940, Mother enrolled at the University of Arizona and took up residency in Tucson. The move to Arizona seemed to disorient the asthma—the hot, dry air wafting over a landscape of cactus, flat-roofed adobe houses, and Indians rolled-up in blankets inducing the asthma to retreat into some dark, dank corner of Mother's lungs. During her four years at the University of Arizona, Mother pursued an art degree but also other interests such as archery and horsemanship. She excelled at these, particularly the archery, and there is a photograph of Mother in white culottes with bow drawn at a collegiate archery tournament. The appearance of horses, bows and arrows, and perhaps white culottes must have further disoriented the asthma, which remained stupefied and nearly dormant someplace in Mother's lungs. Mother graduated from the University of Arizona in 1944 with a degree in fine arts.

But the asthma gradually adapted to desert life. Mother remained in Tucson after graduation, and the asthma eventually ventured forth to grasp again at Mother's lungs. There were limited employment opportunities in Tucson at the end of the war, so by 1948, Mother had moved to Denver. It was in Denver that Mother met my father, and they were married in 1950. They moved to Los Angeles soon after.

My father was from Pennsylvania, a coal miner's son, and he migrated west during the Depression. While eight other siblings were shivering and scrounging—gaunt-eyed—for food and work in Pennsylvania during the 1930s, my father was sweating—wild-eyed— in the California desert. He worked for mining companies that dug colemanite and other borates out of large holes in the ground on the flat desert floor—or scraped borate crystals off dry lake surfaces found on the desert floor itself. Unlike his father and grandfather before him, though, my father's sweating did not come from shoveling coal or even colemanite—my father mostly sweated at night and on weekends in taverns and rooming houses after spending his weekdays filling in long columns of numbers in ledgers. My father was bright, and his father had put together a few dollars so he could attend six months of business college after high school. My father did not have a degree in fine arts, but he knew about money and numbers and how to balance books. He also knew how to make a living and how to have a good time, and he was doing both as he traveled around the western U.S. balancing books for a finance company in the late '40s, when he met Mother.

Henry and Josephine probably did not know what to make of my father, and I don't think they immediately approved of him. At least that's the sense my father conveyed to me, years later. My father was smart and aggressive but also raised in poor circumstances, and Josephine and Henry had probably hoped for something better. They must have realized, though, that at the age of twenty-nine and underemployed and sickly, their daughter couldn't be too choosy. "At least he is Catholic," they probably told themselves—even if he was Irish.

At first, my father and Mother were friendly, and so five children were born between 1951 and 1959. But Mother's asthma, which had shown some previous acclimation to an arid climate, began to feel comfortable in Los Angeles and crept forth from time to time to test the new surroundings and grasp at Mother's lungs. In response, Mother burned the green Asthmador powder and inhaled the adrenaline chloride. As each of the five children was born, Mother burned more of the green Asthmador powder and inhaled the adrenaline chloride more frequently. According to my father, he and Mother eventually went to the priest to see about birth control, and the priest said it was out of the question. This was probably a good thing, because I always appreciated having younger sisters.

When we were young, my father took us out. He would take us to restaurants and to shop for clothes, but also to hike in the mountains and swim at the beach. He often took us to a large, public swimming pool near our house where we would spend most of a summer weekend day frolicking in the water. At first, Mother would accompany us to restaurants or out shopping for clothes, but not to the mountains or beach. Sometimes she would take us shopping or to a restaurant by herself, and she had fine tastes. Occasionally she took us to a museum or art gallery, and she even put her fine arts degree to work by sketching one or more of us in pastels or charcoal. She could draw and even paint, and she was working as a graphic artist in Denver when she met my father.

I don't know when the first ship arrived. I never saw any saucers or discs and I don't remember any green men hanging around the house. They must have come at night while I was asleep, and they probably didn't first arrive until the early 1960s, at about the time Mother decided to stay home. Mother also stopped driving the family car at this time, lost interest in most of our daily activities, no longer went with us to

Mass, and spent more and more time by herself. Often, she would sit alone in her bedroom or in a chair in the living room, staring silently out into space. After a while, she began to talk absently or to converse with someone no one else could see, and sometimes she spoke spontaneously to no one in particular in an agitated manner. One afternoon, as I watched her stare blankly out the window mouthing words silently to herself, it finally occurred to me—she was speaking to someone somewhere in a language I did not know. This was shortly after my brother brought home a book about UFO sightings, and just after I had seen a show on television about a man from Mars with three eyes—the third eye in the center of his forehead where he kept it mostly hidden with a hat. I decided then that the someone Mother was speaking to was likely from a place like Mars.

My father told me later that when Mother first left us, he took her to a psychiatrist. My father said the psychiatrist told him Mother was crazy, but Mother told my father that the psychiatrist was crazy. With a split decision and a house full of children, my father decided Mother should be left at home to keep an eye on us as best she could, or maybe he hoped we would keep an eye on her as best we could. Anyway, my father had to work and support the family, and he must have thought he didn't have a lot of options. If Mother was indeed crazy, the prognosis wasn't good—the only acceptable crazy people in the early 60's were the wealthy who, if truly crazy, were called eccentric. My father and Mother did not have the assets to be considered eccentric.

Thus began twenty-five years of living with Mother and her Martian friends. I never actually saw a Martian and I don't believe my brother or sisters ever saw one either, but I'm not sure any of us would have said so if we did. Contact between Mother and the Martians was probably erratic at first, and it may have taken some time to get the connection working properly, because Mother seemed to switch back and forth frequently from our world to theirs. At some point, Mother may have wanted us all talking to the Martians, because I remember a rare family outing to the planetarium at Griffith Park one evening to learn about the planets. I'm not sure how the connection between the Martians and Mother actually worked, but it probably was accomplished by some kind of mind travel, because she rarely left the house. It's also possible Mother slipped out late at night and visited the Martians in their saucer, because we were all sound sleepers, though there were hazards—like a strong Santa Ana blowing their ship into power lines. If the Martians made regular stops at our house, they were certainly elusive, because my brother and I and my sisters were often out late at night running the streets as we got older. There were reports of UFO sightings all across the western U.S. during the 1960s and '70s, so the Martians were probably out roaming around and visiting others besides Mother.

With time, the relationship between Mother and the Martians impacted all of us. My father started to drink more, Mother's asthma was emboldened, and we children were left to fend for ourselves. The house descended into a state of disorder, Mother became alien to us, and my father became frustrated and angry. Mother and the Martians kept odd hours—Mother often sleeping most of the day, prowling the house at night, and cooking or even cleaning at peculiar intervals. Mother would also alternate long periods of lethargy with short, highly active periods—these active periods often frenzied bouts of scribbling or note-taking or searching for something she couldn't find. From time to time police cars appeared in front of our house, summoned by Mother to report some object stolen that she actually had misplaced. She sometimes accused us of hiding her things, particularly when an object she reported stolen to the police appeared later somewhere in the house. At one point, I wondered if the Martians were borrowing some of these objects, using a transport beam to pass them up to their ship in the night. But the only objects I ever saw flying around our house where those flung by Mother at my father, when he made fun of her. By 1970, Mother had become famous in the neighborhood for the police visits, her loud and incoherent rants on the telephone to neighbors, and her periodic night strolls in a trench coat—among other things. I think the night strolls occurred when she was having trouble contacting her

Martians friends—she apparently lost their signal at times and would go out at night to restore the link.

Mother's asthma seemed to benefit from her relationship with the Martians. Because mind travel required Mother to assume a trance-like state, her asthma would often activate as her body sat limply in the chair. Within a few years of moving to California, the Asthmador powder was providing no help to her at all, and so more adrenaline chloride and then even stronger drugs were administered. She made periodic trips to the hospital when she took too many drugs, but she always returned home after a few days, dried-out and more lucid. Mother fought hard with the asthma, and Mother was a formidable and tenacious foe. But the battle took its toll—Mother became gaunt, stooped, and frail—a blank stare or, on occasion, a fiery glare emanating from her deep-set eyes.

Neither asthma nor the Martians could ever completely control Mother. You would know this because her fine arts degree would occasionally flare up, and some of those flare-ups are the good memories today. It was during these flare-ups that Mother might sketch something, usually one of us children or more than one of us, and she might even talk to us in a coherent manner. Sometimes she would recall something from childhood or from her life before she married, and she would tell us about it, and I realize now that these were some of the few times we ever were able to connect with her. Mother also liked to make artistic arrangements of things, usually in some specific pattern, and she could be very particular about how and where she wanted objects in an arrangement placed. I don't think Mother ever took dance or ballet, but there was even an awkward waltz one night involving Mother, my father, and a butcher knife. I don't remember who took the first step, but there were some quick movements across the kitchen floor, followed by some grappling and jerking and swinging about. I saw drops of blood across the top of Mother's knuckles after they finished, though I missed most of the performance because I was in a closet crying with my sisters.

As my brother and I and my oldest sister entered our teens, Mother would still make occasional trips to the department stores. These trips were mostly to just look, but every once in a while, she would bring home something for one of us to wear. I think the department stores reminded Mother of her early career as a graphic artist drawing department store ads, and she liked the glamour and excitement of seeing cases of jewelry and perfume and the mannequins dressed up in the new styles. I remember she asked me twice to drive her into downtown Los Angeles to drop her off at the department stores along Broadway, and then pick her up at a place she specified three or four hours later. She was a haunting figure as she strode along on the sidewalk, a long coat worn over one of her ancient, sweeping dresses—coal-dark eyes peering out of a cadaverous face. Still, Mother enjoyed these trips and would chatter happily about what she saw in the stores as we drove home later in the car. I still have a jacket Mother bought for me nearly forty years ago from one of these shopping trips.

Mother left this earth for good in the autumn of 1986. All her children were grown, and her last years were spent by herself at home with my father. The asthma took an ever firmer grip on her lungs during this period, and she spent nearly all her time in mind-travel. Toward the end, though, I think the mind-travel ceased after a series of small strokes and, at the end, I don't think her mind was connected to much of anything at all. At the time, I was living north of Los Angeles, and I drove down one evening after one of her hospital stays to check on her at the house. She was in bed and needed a bath. My father was well advanced into his own health problems, but the two of us were able to get her up and into the bathroom and bathe her. It was the only time I ever bathed one of my parents. It was a horror and a privilege.

My mother died in a rest home two weeks later. I don't know if the mother ship came for her, but if it did, she didn't go. A mother of a different sort came, and I know this because of her appearance in the box. Though twenty-five years of mind-travel and a lifetime of asthma had left my mother broken and sick, the life drained out of her, there was a viewing before the funeral, the casket was open, and she looked better than I could ever recall. She was wearing one of her long, sweeping dresses and her face was the one I had seen in a wedding photograph taken thirty-six years before. Being greeted by our Blessed Mother is the only thing that could have made my mother look this way.

My father died three months after my mother, just before Christmas. He wasn't ready to go, and he resisted. The funeral was on my birthday, and he looked horrible in the box. I pray for him and my mother every day. I still worry about my father.

# The Sunset Program

These had been difficult years. The last five had been the hardest, since her husband died and she was left to care for their daughter, Missy, by herself. At her husband's death, there was no longer any pension, and so she had gone on the dole to provide for Missy's support. There still wasn't much improvement in Missy since her accident, just occasional winks or a few rapid bats of the eye—though she would occasionally smile suddenly without provocation. It would be over soon, now, Missy's mother had been assured. The case worker from the Health Enhancement Department was sending out a nurse and doctor, accompanied by police officers from the Bureau of Civil Harmony, to disconnect Missy from life support. The priest would be present and Missy's attorney would also come, but all appeals had been exhausted and the Health Enhancement Department had a court order. It was half past one in the afternoon and by half past three, Missy would be gone. Not just from the realm of the living, but also physically removed from the house.

Missy's case worker from the Health Enhancement Department was an older woman with a bad limp. The woman joked that she couldn't walk right and needed a hip replacement, but that everything else about her was in top shape. She had never married and had no children—or at least none she had carried to term. She was a cheerful woman with gray hair, merry blue eyes, and a medium set. She also had remarkably smooth and youthful-looking skin—everyone noticed it—which she attributed to careful eating habits and a special cream she had applied to her skin for the past twenty-five years. Missy's case worker had been an early supporter of the program that was to terminate Missy's life— called The Sunset Program—and one of its most enthusiastic promoters. She fancied herself on the cutting edge of new thought and progressive ideas, and felt a certain thrill when one of these thoughts or ideas was actualized. She had been on the cutting edge of new thought and new ideas for most of her fifty-three years. One reason she was made the local director of The Sunset Program was because she could be counted upon to be enthusiastic and articulate about its implementation. The other reason was that no one else wanted the job—there was still some reticence about killing the sick and disabled.

New thought and new ideas don't always arrive easily, however, and it had taken ten years for the law that instituted The Sunset Program to be fully implemented. There had been legal challenges and even civil disturbances but, finally, there had been enough financial incentives offered to lawmakers to push the program through. The woman with the limp said this was a sign of positive change and of the new thinking so desperately needed in the country. The woman with the limp viewed herself as a change agent.

The crew from the Health Enhancement Department arrived promptly at two, after the priest had come and then Missy's attorney. All of them sat uncomfortably in the small living room of Missy's home, with Missy lying nearby in her large hospital bed. There was then an awkward wait for the two officers from the Bureau of Civil Harmony, during which the older woman with the limp tried to ease the situation by talking about the weather and then about something called the Fuel Usage Tax Credit Program. The woman with the limp was from Minnesota and found the weather in Texas warm. She cited a government study that reported a temperature rise of a degree and a quarter in Houston over the past thirty-five years to support her claim that the weather was becoming even warmer. The woman with the limp said this was unacceptable, and declared that she had been an avid supporter of the Fuel Usage Tax Credit Program since it was first unveiled, and that this program would reverse the rise in temperature. As it turned out, there weren't actually any tax credits associated with the Fuel Usage Tax Credit Program—only penalties for exceeding a monthly energy usage allocation. But the program did force ever more people onto the bus system or riding bicycles. The Fuel Usage Tax Credit Program had also caused an increase in home fires and respiratory problems during the previous two winters—which had been cooler than usual—as people resorted to burning wood, garbage, or even dried horse and cow dung to heat their homes. One other unforeseen outcome of the Fuel Usage Tax Credit Program was that more of the elderly and those with chronic lung problems were qualifying for The Sunset Program—because of respiratory distress—which rendered the woman with the limp feeling even more fulfilled.

Finally, at fifteen to three, the woman with the limp asked if anyone had a deck of cards. Missy's attorney thought this was incredibly insensitive and said so, after which the woman with the limp took the occasion to quietly threaten the attorney, whom she already had disbarred. Still, the older woman backed away from the card idea, as everyone continued to sit around looking at each other. "Where are the police when you need them?" the older woman with the limp finally said with a laugh. Then the woman addressed the priest, who along with Missy's mother was fingering a rosary, and said, "So much of the Christian message is so beautiful, and yet it is such a pity that so much of it is mired in backwardness and superstition. Think of all the good the churches could do if they were more aligned with the government and progressive thought."

"What's progressive about killing the disabled?" replied the priest.

"See, now there you go. You're not looking at the big picture. The world would be a better place with a healthy, robust population—free of sickness and disease."

The priest turned silent, having gone down this course of conversation with the woman with the limp before. The woman with the limp then embarked on a related topic, mentioning that she had signed a consent form—called the Organ Recycling Consent Form— that allowed her various body parts to be donated to organ banks upon the event of her demise. The woman also commented that wouldn't it be smart if everyone did this, so that younger people with serious maladies could acquire replacement organs and live long, productive lives. Missy's attorney had not allowed Missy's mother to ever sign the Organ Recycling Consent Form, either on behalf of Missy or on behalf of herself, and was appalled that such a topic was even being mentioned by the woman with the limp. But being a progressive, even the most awkward subjects fell within the older woman's range.

Finally, upon reaching another lull in the conversation and being someone to never waste the opportunity to fill it, particularly with herself, the older woman began to talk about her hip. "I should be getting a hip replacement this year. I've been on the list for six years and it looks like it will be my turn in November. Of course, it could get moved up. You have to be ready at almost a moment's notice. Sometimes there's a cancelation and they want to do it that day. These hip operations are another miracle of modern medicine."

At four o'clock, the woman with the limp became uneasy. The doctor that came with her was on call but the nurse would be on overtime if events lasted much past five, and the older woman prided herself on managing a smooth, cost-efficient operation. She then put in her second call of the afternoon to Health Enhancement Department Headquarters, only to be advised that Headquarters was aware of the situation but that something unexpected had come up. The woman with the limp was assured that assistance would soon be on the way. The woman then found it necessary to say, "I've never experienced a delay like this in any previous sunsetting that I've done. I apologize for the wait."

At four-thirty, a police car from the Bureau of Civil Harmony and an ambulance appeared at the front of the house. Four police officers, another doctor and nurse, and two ambulance attendants were soon standing in the living room of the house. After dismissing the doctor and nurse already in attendance, the new doctor addressed the woman with the limp, saying, "There's been a change in plans, Ms. Gage. I'll be in charge now, and we need to finish here quickly."

"Oh, yes, I'm all for that. This has already gone on too long—I have a budget and I don't want to pay any overtime," replied the woman with the limp.

"Before we start, Ms. Gage, I want to ask a few questions."

"Of course."

"How are you feeling, Ms. Gage?"

"Oh, quite well."

"You certainly look well—the picture of health," and the new doctor nodded to his nurse. "You certainly have nice skin—I haven't seen such clear, bright skin on a woman your age in a long time."

"Well, thank you! I take my health seriously. Only pure, natural foods and supplements for me, and I use a special skin cream every day—YouthBlend Edge—it has aloe and vitamin E and a moisturizer made from fetal skin cells that…"

"Very well, Ms. Gage. Nurse Blount, would you take Ms. Gage's vitals?"

"Vitals? What for?" inquired the woman with the limp.

"We have a surprise for you, Ms. Gage. You qualify for a program that you enrolled in some time ago."

"Oh, my! I can't believe it. Finally!"

The nurse nodded at the doctor after taking Ms. Gage's vitals. The new doctor had come with medical information on a small computer and was quickly scanning it. Then the nurse prepared an injection. Two of the officers from the Bureau of Civil Harmony pounced quickly on Ms. Gage and the nurse gave the woman the needle.

"No need to hold me! Who do you think I am? I've waited a long time for this hip."

"Hip?" replied the doctor.

"You're here to take me for hip replacement surgery, correct? I'm due this year."

"We're not here for your hip—just for your spleen and kidneys. The Vice President flew into town yesterday to give a speech, but ended up at the hospital with kidney failure. He's had weak kidneys for years and you were the best, short-notice donor we could find. You may be fifty-three, but the Vice President is almost seventy and he should be able to go another ten years with your spleen and kidneys."

"Now wait a minute…" began the woman with the limp, but she was already beginning to slur her words after the injection."You can't just come and take my spleen and kidneys."

"You gave us permission."

"I did not!"

"Yes, you did—when you signed the Organ Recycling Consent Form."

"But I'm still alive."

"Don't worry—you'll be dead soon."

"There must be some mistake…" and the woman with the limp began to lose consciousness. She then revived for a few moments, and shrieked to Missy's lawyer, "Stop this! Don't let them do this!"

The lawyer shrugged, "You had me disbarred, remember? There's nothing I can do."

"Get her on a gurney and let's get out of here. We don't have much time," the doctor said to the ambulance attendants.

"She didn't read the fine print?" queried Missy's lawyer.

"Who are you?"

"The lawyer for the family."

"Then you should know that when you sign papers donating organs, the government has the option of seizing the organs in a state emergency—a right of eminent domain. The Vice President had an emergency and we located Ms. Gage as soon as we could, though it took a while to sort everything out and get over here to pick her up."

"And what about Missy?" inquired the lawyer, motioning to the girl in the hospital bed.

"I wouldn't worry too much about her. One purpose of The Sunset Program was to access the organs of those who refuse to sign the Organ Recycling Consent Form. Many of her organs are probably atrophied and not much good to anyone anyway. I don't know why Ms. Gage was so anxious to sunset her—though someone said it allowed her to reach an early quota and qualify for a cruise to Alaska. It's nice in Alaska this time of year—70 degrees and no humidity."

"Then Missy is safe."

"For now—yes. I'll take her off the list. Actually, replacing her with a better donor like Ms. Gage gives our department a credit."

So the old lady with the limp was wheeled out. Then Missy winked and blinked, smiled suddenly, and uttered her first word in twelve years. A new kidney and spleen were soon installed in the Vice President, who lived another year before having a massive heart attack. Besides a spleen and kidneys, Ms. Gage also parted with her eyes, her liver, her good hip, and four feet of small intestine. Her heart was given to some animal rights people who had it quickly transplanted into a sick research chimpanzee, where it beat for nine minutes before the chimpanzee expired. Some of the rest of Ms. Gage ended up in glass jars on shelves in medical schools, though parts of her were also shoveled into a box and taken out to the dumpster after they spilled off the table onto the concrete floor of the operating room. Missy's priest soon had Missy enrolled in a new program he had started for Missy and a few others like her—it was called The Sunrise Program.

Missy and her mother haven't heard anything from the Health Enhancement Department in seven years, and Missy can now speak in simple sentences. The government checks keep coming, arriving on the fourth of every month. The government never had to pay the doctors, nurses, police officers, ambulance attendants, or the old lady with the limp any overtime.

# Time Traveler

His wristwatch read four o'clock. This was then confirmed by the large pedestal clock in the foyer, which began to sound out the hour. In another hour, he could leave and no one would think it too soon. It might even be good if he left first—he had come alone and so an early departure would be understandable as well as a signal to the others that they too could soon leave. Though he had someplace to be later, he was only on his second drink. He felt comfortable surrounded by old friends, and had yet to try any of the food.

"Can I freshen your drink, Stan?" inquired Tammy, as he remained stalled in his chair.

"Yes, please."

"Well, you all came—Sam is just tickled that you all made it again."

"We've done this now for so many years—it's a tradition. I think we all look forward to it."

"Sam certainly enjoys it. Look at him—you would think he was eighteen-years-old or something."

Sam was standing beside Jason and across from Steven and Kenny, laughing and gesturing by the side of the pool. Portly and tan, Sam seemed particularly animated and flushed.

"Sam is feeling well, Tammy?"

"Yes, I think so. He has to watch himself, though. Or, more correctly, I've got to watch him. I have to watch his diet and make sure he doesn't overdo it. He'll pay for this tomorrow—he'll be weak and tired. But he so enjoys this. I'm so glad you could all come."

"Well, I'm happy to be here."

They had all started out building houses over thirty years ago. Construction on the coast was beginning to boom, and they all migrated down from the north to make their fortunes. They came from different towns in different states and did not know each other at first, but within six months they were friends and helping on each other's houses. If one of them was in a tight spot and needed a plumber, the other would send his plumber over to help. If one of them ran short of plywood to finish out a garage, one of the others would send over the wood. Back then, they didn't keep track of hours or men or the time and supplies loaned to each other—they shared subcontractors and materials and even worked on each others' houses. Once a week, they met on the beach in the evening with a keg and some girls and their lives, though busy, were uncomplicated. With the exception of Stan, each of them married a local girl they met on the beach. Each one's word was their contract and they could keep their word.

But the business of building houses changed and so did the men building the houses. Sam became a developer and stopped building his own houses. Kenny also became a developer, specializing in apartments. Jason formed a company to build all of Sam's houses and condominiums and all of Kenny's apartments, as well as houses and apartments and condominiums for other developers. Steven had three sons and together they began building custom houses—the large, expensive kind. Only Stan still built houses by himself, one or two at a time. He still swung a hammer and pushed a saw, even if lately he depended more on his nail gun and the pre-cut wood he ordered from the lumber yard. Stan also was the only one to move back north, after only five years, and so he had not benefited from the prolonged surge of construction on the coast.

Words had also changed. Not all of them had been able to keep their word, and there had been lawsuits and litigation and out of court settlements. Now, elaborate written contracts were required to make sure everyone kept their word. Because words had changed, only five of them now met each year instead of the original seven, and most of the five no longer had their original wives but had married new girls from the beach. These new girls, like Tammy, were now in their late thirties with bleached hair and spiked heels and spreading thighs and breasts crammed tightly into shiny leather or reflective lycra. Only Steven and his wife had stayed together and were together this afternoon. Stan would have stayed with his wife, but she made other plans and left with the children. Despite everything, the remaining five were all still friends and none of them had done enough to one of the others to break that friendship. And so they met and mingled as they had done every year on twenty-five previous Saturday afternoons in May at the coast.

"The shuttle should be visible tonight," Jason was saying as Stan approached Sam and the other men.

"Oh really! I should get out my telescope," said Sam.

"It will be landing at the Cape and will pass overhead just before eight o'clock," continued Jason. "There should be a moving light in the sky—unless the sun sets too soon and there's no reflection."

"Well, here's Stan. He's the space expert. Will the shuttle be visible tonight?" inquired Sam.

"I think so. It should be visible if the angle's right."

"Well, there you have it. Stan's word has always been pretty good," and they all bobbed their heads in agreement.

"That must be a heck of a ride," began Kenny.

"You said it—I wonder what that must be like," added Jason.

"I read someplace that if you get going fast enough, time stands still. Or at least slows down," continued Kenny. "I think Einstein came up with that. That would be something, wouldn't it? I wonder what time standing still would be like? What if you could get it to go backwards?"

Stan shook his head and muttered quietly. Then the others began talking among themselves and speculating on what traveling fast enough to suspend time would be like. Steven then took Stan by the elbow and guided him off to the side.

"Say, Stan, are you still building houses up in Longview?" Steven began.

"Yep, got two going now."

"You know that lake up there—Pritchard Reservoir—have you built any houses on it?"

"I built one last year. It's kind of a high-end development—big lots with some great views. Actually, the sort of thing you and your sons might be interested in. You should come up and have a look."

"I might do that. The coast is overbuilt. It's saturated and expensive and I'm looking to branch out—start something new for my boys. I might even do a spec house or two."

"How are the boys?"

"Good—real good. They're such a God-send. I can't be thankful enough for my sons."

Stan nodded.

"Say, Stan, did you come down with Margie? I thought I saw her in Buster's last night. How are your children, anyway?"

"It couldn't have been Margie—I came down by myself. My kids are fine, I think. I don't see them much—except for my boy. He works with me in the summer."

"I could have sworn that was Margie last night—but then I haven't seen her in seven or eight years. You're probably right—it was someone else."

"Probably so," Stan confirmed. "But I expect to see them this next week—my youngest is graduating." He almost let it slip that he might see them even sooner, but that would be a complicated story and hard to explain.

Half an hour later, Stan was shaking hands on a farewell sweep through Sam's house. Like in other years, Steven and his wife had offered Stan lodging for the night at their home, but Stan had made other arrangements. He had stayed up the coast at a certain motel on a bluff overlooking the beach for the past five years. Like Sam's party, the motel had also become a sort of tradition. He was suddenly anxious to go.

It was almost six when Stan turned the key to his room. He carried an overnight bag on his shoulder and a cardboard box in his arms. The bag held a change of clothes and the box held, among other things, his liquor and some food. Stan laid his bag on the bed in the bedroom, and then went to the living area where a sliding glass door opened onto a balcony. The curtain was drawn and the sun was low on the horizon, about to fall through a layer of thin clouds. These were the only clouds in the sky, and the sea glistened and shimmered in the light from the sun. There was a cone of particularly bright light that spread out from the sun, across the water to the shore—almost too bright to look at without hurting your eyes. Stan stood at the slider with the box in his arms, gazing at the sun.

Stan had always been interested in the sun and the planets, in the stars and everything else celestial. As a child he had wanted to be an astronaut, and his father would wake him early to watch the liftoffs of space vehicles from Cape Canaveral on television. Stan knew all about the Gemini missions and the Apollo flights, and he could name the astronauts on each flight and tell something about them personally. Stan had kept plastic replicas of various spacecraft hanging on strings from his bedroom ceiling, and pasted posters of the planets and the sun on his bedroom wall. He and three other boys formed an astronomy club in high school, and he planned to study aeronautics in college. But there was no money for college, and so three days after his high school graduation, he went to work with his dad. His dad did remodeling and together they worked over about twenty homes and businesses in a two year span. Then his father fell through a rotted second story floor and broke his back. His father never walked again, and Stan went south to the coast where he heard construction was booming and there was money to be made. In five years, Stan made enough money to clear his father's medical bills. Then his father died and Stan moved back north for his mother. There was also a girl from home he wanted to marry, and two years later they started their family.

Stan never forgot his friends from the coast and would drive down for a week early every summer with his wife. They would camp on the beach in tents at a facility run by the state and get together once or twice with Sam, Steven, and the others. Stan's wife, Kate, did not take to Stan's friends, particularly the wives, but Kate had never seen the ocean and the clear, green sea. So they spent most of their days on the beach laying about on the bright, white sand or frolicking in the clear, green water. As their children were born, each of them also made the annual pilgrimage to the coast and soon Stan, Kate and their children were playing happily in the green sea and building castles and forts in the white sand. These were almost magical days, and there came a lightness and excitement that they felt at almost no other time or place. They still stopped in to see Stan's friends at least once on their annual visit south, but these became more awkward as Stan's friends became affluent and changed wives. After ten years of traveling south, Stan was visiting his friends either alone or with just one or two of his children—Kate and the other children preferring to remain at the campground with the tents.

On the eleventh year of their annual southward migration, Kate announced it would be her last. Stan saved money and finally talked Kate into going a twelfth year and staying at a motel, and that was how Stan found the motel with the room he was standing in now. There was enough money that twelfth year to stay four nights at the motel and, until five years ago, he had not been back. Though Kate grumbled about making the long trip to the coast for just four days, all of them probably had their best beach trip ever. Kate seemed hesitant and almost wistful on the morning they had to return home, but she never made the trip again. Stan continued to come every year and camp, sometimes with his son, but that ended when Kate left six years ago. Now he always stayed at the motel.

The motel had thirty-six units, including an original row of eight bungalows built of cinder block dating to the 1950s. There was a second, newer building with sixteen units, eight on each floor. The third building was newer still and held twelve units on three floors. Stan had never stayed in the bungalows, nor had he stayed in the three-story building. He always stayed in the second building because it was located directly on the bluff overlooking the beach, and he always stayed on the second floor. When he had come with Kate and their children for four nights thirteen years ago, they also stayed on the second floor. Stan could not remember for sure which room they stayed in during that visit, but it was either the third or fourth unit from the east end. He had stayed in both these units at least once over the past five years. Though Stan pretended it didn't matter which room he stayed in, as long as it was on the second floor, he was a little disappointed this year to find himself in the end room beside the pool. All the second floor rooms were laid out the same and were identical except for this end room, which had two side windows that overlooked the pool and bungalows. Most visitors would have been pleased to get the end room because of the windows and view, but not Stan.

The sun now rested on the clouds along the horizon. Stan had remained standing at the slider, looking out at the ocean and sun, but now began to move about. His room was an efficiency that included a sink and small stove and a refrigerator, and he quickly put away his small cache of food. He next turned on the stereo inside the television cabinet, before pulling binoculars from his cardboard box and setting them on a table beside the slider. He also retrieved two plastic, miniature

Apollo space capsules from the cardboard box and hung them from the ceiling on strings he tied to the metal air vents, using a bar stool to reach the vents. Then he activated the ceiling fan and the Apollo capsules began rotating slowly in large arcs, propelled by air currents from the fan. Finally, he got into his liquor and opened the bag of ice he bought fifteen minutes earlier at the market on the town square just down from the motel, and mixed his first drink. Almost as an afterthought, he set the alarm on his wristwatch.

After sipping half of his first drink, Stan went back to the bedroom and changed clothes. He stepped into gray sweat pants, pulled on a T-shirt, and then threw on an old black, hooded, cotton jacket. He returned to the small kitchen and mixed a second and third drink, placing them beside his binoculars on the table just inside from the slider. He opened the slider and sat down on a bar stool that he placed with two legs inside the room and the other two on the balcony outside. He always used a bar stool for this because it allowed him to sit high and see over the balcony rail to the beach and waves below. From this location, he could also hear the stereo above the sound of the wind buffeting over the balcony.

He finished his second drink and started the third. He watched the shore birds peck along the edge of the water, the pelicans glide in long sweeps above the waves, and the last few walkers trek down the beach. He picked up his binoculars and spotted two or three porpoises—way out in the water. With his drinks, his binoculars, and the sound of the wind coursing over the balcony as the stereo played in the background, Stan relaxed. Dusk was coming on and soon he would go out to walk.

Stan left his room that evening at half-past seven. He descended the outdoor stairway to the first floor walkway, and started out across the carefully manicured lawn toward the edge of the bluff overlooking the beach. The lawn was a short, smooth, Bermuda grass lawn and he always marveled at how even and perfect it seemed to be. In the center of the lawn was a still, clear pool and it always pained him to see it this way. He remembered his children swimming and playing in this pool, splashing and scooting about. He thought this pool should always have someone in it, so the water would be moving, and it wouldn't be so blue and still. He quickly reached the far edge of the lawn, where there was a wooden gazebo at the top of a long flight of stairs that fell down the bluff to the beach.

It was breezy in the gazebo as he lingered there. He managed to light one of his infrequent cigars, and puffed on it as he gazed up and down the beach. This had become a favorite place of his, but he would not be alone for long. Other smokers came here to puff and look, and it was the main access from the beach to the motel. The gazebo was about thirty feet above the beach, and from this vantage he could look out a long way in either direction along the shoreline, as well as back across the lawn to the pool and buildings. About three miles to the west, where some faint lights now appeared, was the campground where he, Kate, and the children had always stayed. To the east, the beach gradually curved along the bluff for two or three miles toward a single, tall, vertical stack of condominiums sprouting upward from the dunes. Directly south, an immense expanse of sea spread out ahead of him. Stan sucked hard on his cigar. Then, glancing about quickly, he brought out a flask from inside his jacket and opened it and took a swallow. He swallowed again, and again sucked hard on his cigar. Looking around a final time, he put his hood up and raised the zipper on his coat. His body felt light and he had a floating sensation, and it was time for his walk.

Stan was lightheaded as he started down the long flight of stairs. He dropped quickly, almost effortlessly, as gravity pulled him toward the bottom. The stairs were aluminum stairs, replacing the previous wooden steps swept away by the last hurricane. His feet made a pinging sound as he bounced downward, two and three steps at a time. Last year, he gained so much momentum going down these stairs that he lost his footing and became airborne near the bottom—careening off the rail and out into space before sprawling awkwardly onto the sand. Later, as he recalled this incident, he laughed and referred to it as his "spacewalk." This year, though, Stan resolved to avoid the same outcome.

Quickly reaching the beach at the base of the stairs, Stan drove both feet into the sand and remained upright. Then, stumbling and staggering, he began to slog out across the sand. The sun now lingered on the horizon behind the clouds, and occasionally a shaft of light would find a slit in the clouds, sending a bright beam to the beach. These shafts of light would alternate with denser, darker periods when the sun lay hidden behind the clouds, illuminating them from behind. Stan reached the shoreline and stopped there, puffing some more on his cigar. He swallowed again from his flask. It was a spectacular sunset.

Then the alarm on his watch went off. Startled for a moment, Stan silenced the alarm and gazed skyward. He searched for several minutes before he saw it—a faint light traveling quickly from west to east, about midway up from the horizon. It was the space shuttle, on descent to its landing at the Cape. Gazing back out westward from where the shuttle had come, he continued to walk.

The wind was blowing out of the southwest and directly into his face. He pulled the drawstrings of his hood and tied them tightly beneath his chin. The walking was easier on the hard, wet sand near the water's edge, so he trekked west along this wet edge. He decided that he had drunk enough, and needed only the remainder of his cigar to propel him along. It was important that he not drink too much and repeat the incident of three years earlier. That time, he drank so much that he finally had to sit down on the sand. And soon, before he knew it, he had lain down on the sand. Then time slowed down, there was a sensation of floating backwards, and not even Einstein could have predicted what happened next. Because, suddenly, they were all together—he, Kate, and their children—all of them laughing and playing on the beach. It was one of those bright, blue, magical days when the sea was clear and green and the white sand seemed whiter than usual. But then, in an instant, it turned dark and he felt cold and damp. His head was spinning and he yelled something, before flailing about on the sand and finding his feet and pants wet. Sitting up quickly, he saw waves breaking a few yards away and realized the tide had rolled in.

As another breaker had rolled toward him, Stan jumped up off the sand. He retreated several steps toward the bluff, and found himself on a black and empty beach. There was a bad taste in his mouth and his head hurt but, for a moment, there remained a fleeting image of Kate and his children. He wanted to keep this image alive, but he was suddenly sick to his stomach and the image vanished and then he could not re-animate or reconnect to it. He eventually slogged back down the beach and up the wooden stairs to the motel. He almost never remembered his dreams— he thought for a long time that he never had any—but found afterwards that he could recall parts of this one and they were as vivid as anything he had ever experienced awake. At the core of the dream was Kate and his children—particularly his children—and for weeks afterwards he was haunted by the memory of it. Now when he came to the coast and took his evening walk along the beach, he knew not to drink too much. He did not want to risk a severing of whatever connection he might be able to establish. This connection was a tether that, whenever intact, felt like a lifeline.

And so, this particular evening, he continued his walk westward along the beach. He finished his cigar and threw the stub into the water. He noticed the slow rise of the tide and watched the white tops of the waves curl and break as they ran diagonally toward the beach. He waited for time to slow down and the memories to flood up, like they had on this walk in previous years, but nothing happened. He walked three miles to where there was a wooden ramp over the dunes. He knew this ramp because it led to the campground and facilities where he and his family had always camped. He climbed the ramp to the top of the dunes and waited there, gazing into space, until he noticed the planet Venus as a bright speck on the western horizon near a sliver of moon. He was suddenly hopeful, because there was a particular memory associated with this ramp on another evening when Venus was visible—an evening many years ago when his two youngest children walked down this ramp arm in arm, singing. It was unusual for his two youngest to break out in spontaneous song, particularly with arms interlocked, but they had done so that evening. But even this memory was faint tonight and he could not conjure up their voices. The only sound was the wind and the slow drum of the waves. He turned back.

For twenty-five years, he had made this annual trip to the coast to visit his old friends. For the past five years, he had made a point of walking this beach at dusk until the memories began to flood back. But memories were elusive this night, and he walked back toward the motel without being able to retrieve much more than a few fleeting glimpses of the past.

After two miles, Stan climbed up off the beach on one of the stairways that led directly into the town. It wasn't a big town—an arc of shops and restaurants around a plaza shaped in a half-circle. Surrounding the shops and restaurants were summer cottages, probably a couple of hundred of them, with more added every year. Most of the cottages were high-end places, and the automobiles parked outside had plates from Georgia, the Carolinas, and even New England. These were custom-built cottages, the kind Steven and his sons put up, and over the last several years he had observed nine or ten of these cottages with one of Steven's signs posted outside. Sam and the others had never ventured into this kind of development—it was not the sort of mass-produced construction for which they were suited.

The town had been a familiar place to Stan and his family. Every year they had come south to the coast, they would spend at least one afternoon strolling through this town, stopping for ice cream and to look at the cottages or to cruise about on one of the pedal carts. There was one place, years ago, where someone set up a miniature train. The train was there for only two or three years, but one of those years Stan came down with just his son and bought four tickets at five dollars apiece, so his son could make sixteen loops riding the miniature train along rails lain through the brush and sand. The train had a whistle and was rigged to send smoke through its stack, and Stan had walked through town each of the past five years trying to recall the tone of that whistle. This evening, though, he paused only briefly to look at the place—now a row of shops—where once his son rode the train.

It was now almost ten o'clock and Stan was tired. He would be leaving tomorrow, but part of his yearly routine was to make a quick walk through the main part of town and stop for coffee at the market where earlier he had bought his ice. If it wasn't too late, he would then linger a while before walking the two lane road back to the motel. Stan found the market closed, so he made for an ice cream parlor that also served coffee. Reaching the entryway to the ice cream parlor, he stumbled into his two youngest daughters.

"Oh my!" said Margie, the older of the two. "I didn't expect to see you here!"

Stan stammered for a reply. "I'm down to see Sam Landers and some of my old contractor friends. You remember—we'd get together every year about this time and spend an afternoon with them. I'm here for that."

"Oh yes, I remember. They were nice people," replied Margie.

"It's sure good to see you two—it's been a while."

"Like six years," retorted Lisa.

"Your brother says you both are doing well."

"Yes, we're fine," the two young women replied in unison. "We came down for a few days before the rates go up," added Margie.

"Your brother says Margie has a serious boyfriend!" Stan suddenly blurted, desperate for something to say.

"Oh Lord! That's Luke and his big mouth," said Margie.

The conversation lulled a moment, the three of them searching for words. Then Stan gestured and said, "Let's sit down for just a minute— here's a table and chairs."

"No, we have to get back. Louise is waiting for us and I have to work tomorrow evening, so this is our last night here. We have to get up early to drive back home."

"Just for a minute? You can't sit for a minute?"

"No—we really should go," repeated Lisa. "Look, we haven't seen you in years—maybe some other time."

"You were hard on him," Margie remarked to Lisa as they walked away. "He never forgot us—he always remembers our birthday and the holidays and sends us things. That counts for something."

"I know. But I didn't know what else to say. This is awkward and it was a surprise to see him."

"Well, I know what to say," and Margie spun around and walked back to Stan, who was watching them.

"Look, Dad, this is unexpected. We aren't trying to be rude, but we're surprised to see you."

"I know that. I'm not trying to push anything on you. I'm coming for Luke's graduation next week—maybe we can visit then."

"Maybe. But it will be difficult with Mother there—she still doesn't want you around. Look, Luke wants to get us all together in three weeks for Father's Day. I don't know about Lisa, but I'll go. Just act surprised, so Luke doesn't know I've talked to you. Luke wants it to be a surprise."

"Oh, I will. Thank You."

"Okay, I'll see you then."

"God Bless you both."

And Margie nodded as she walked away.

Stan waited until they were both in their car, and watched as they drove away. He then went and got his coffee. He was almost skipping as he made his way down the two lane road to his room at the motel, spilling most of the coffee along the way. He turned the key to his room, put on the kitchen light, and took off his cotton jacket. Because he planned to leave early in the morning, he got up on a bar stool and began to unfasten the strings that suspended his miniature space capsules from the vents. Through a side window—a window only his room had because of its position on the corner of the building—he was surprised to see his two daughters in the pool. And not just Margie and Lisa, as it turned out, but Louise and Luke were in the pool as well. It was late, but they were splashing and darting about. The pool was in motion again.

And so Stan unfastened his capsules and got down off the stool. He returned the capsules to their box, lit a lamp way back in the bedroom, and came back and turned off the kitchen light. He opened the side window and slider, and positioned a bar stool with two legs on the balcony and two legs inside. He sat on the stool as a steady breeze swept in from the beach. If he leaned forward on the stool and turned his head to the left, he could see his children in the pool. If he leaned forward and turned right, he could gaze down the beach in the darkness to the place where there had been magical days on the white sand beach with Kate and his children. But mostly he stared straight ahead, out to sea and space, and listened.

He recognized each of his children's voices as they drifted up from the pool. After a while, he leaned forward and looked right and again found the bright speck of Venus above the western horizon, having climbed a little higher. Then there was an early evening fourteen years earlier, when he and his son and youngest daughter went out to watch the sun set over the water at the campground down the beach. They walked the ramp over the dunes to the white sand beach, and stood silently for several minutes as the sky burned and flared in shades of orange, and pink, and grey. After the sky finally darkened, they turned to take the ramp back over the dunes. Then, without warning, his two children began to sing. He could hear their words distinctly, arms locked together, as they walked down the ramp ahead of him. Then the whistle of a train sounded. It came from town. Time stood still.

# Change

"It won't start, sir."

"What?"

"It won't start, Captain—I turn the key and nothing happens."

"What do you mean 'nothing happens'? Novak, you're the mechanic—make something happen!"

Novak said nothing and turned the key again.

"Damn it, Novak! Get this thing moving!"

"I'm trying, sir." Novak turned the key back and forth rapidly in the ignition.

"Novak—damn it! This is the army! Get this truck moving!"

At that moment, the engine fired. The truck heaved forward and almost stalled, Novak having momentarily taken his foot off the clutch with the transmission engaged. There was a scuffling of the captain's feet on the roof overhead as Novak quickly depressed the clutch pedal.

"Novak, you stupid fool! Don't leave the transmission engaged when you're trying to start! You almost threw me off!"

"Yes, sir! Sorry, sir!"

"Shut up, Novak! Just drive!"

Novak quickly released the clutch and the truck bolted forward. Again there was a scuffle of feet along with more shouting from overhead. The truck left the compound and rolled down a slight incline toward a bowl-shaped depression surrounded by a tall fence.  The fence was strung between towers and enclosed wooden barracks. A guard swung open a pair of iron gates as the truck approached the fence.

The truck gained momentum as it rumbled through the gates. Novak attempted to follow the road as it veered to the left, but it had been raining and the ground was soft and slick. The truck began to slide sideways and then slanted off the road, the tires flinging tall arcs of black mud as they churned toward a shallow moat that tightly encircled the wooden barracks. There was a great splash as the truck encountered the moat, and a wave of stinking water leapt forward to slap against a wall of one of the barracks. As the truck came to a halt in the moat, wild laughter came from the roof overhead.

"You crazy fool, Novak! You almost wrecked us!" There was more laughter.

"I'm sorry, sir. It got away from me a little."

"Just a little?" Then another burst of laughter.

"I'm not used to these big trucks, Captain. But I'll get better."

"Oh, there's no hurry—I mean—what a ride!" Then suddenly becoming serious the captain shouted, "I'll bust you for good if you wreck this truck—do you hear me?"

"Yes, Captain."

"And I want that damned ignition fixed! Right away!"

"Yes, Captain."

"Get us out of this mess—now!"

"Yes, Captain."

It was an old truck but the captain felt fortunate to have it. He had a brother in Motor Pool but it had still taken months to get. It was a tall and heavy vehicle, high off the ground, with three axles and enormous tires. It had tanks on the side for fuel and water and a broad, steel bulwark attached to the front. Though the captain could put thirty men in back under the canvass cover, he was more satisfied with the .50-caliber machine gun mounted on a turret on the truck's roof. The captain had been testing various drivers for the past month, but the truck was temperamental and required almost constant tinkering. Novak, though inferior to the other drivers, had so far been the only competent mechanic.

Two gaunt men had come out of the barracks. They watched as Novak jerked the truck roughly out of the moat. Novak was then ordered to speed up, and the truck began to circle the moat and barracks, the tall tires fanning huge sprays of black mud as they churned through the soft ground. The captain crouched on top of the cab, grinning and grunting as he swept his gun exuberantly from side to side. After circling the barracks for several minutes, the captain struck a more dignified pose and ordered the truck to a halt. He then arranged himself behind the gun, assumed an exaggerated composure, and fired a round over the top of the barracks. The gaunt men threw themselves to the ground as the shells passed harmlessly overhead. A flush of satisfaction swept across the captain's face as he barked at Novak and the truck lurched and turned, reaching for the road. The truck then exited through the iron gates and rumbled back toward the compound.

"Foolishness!" said one of the men, as both of them rose off the ground.

"Yes. They want to rule but are themselves unruly. Come on, let's go inside."

"Wait, Henry, we've got to talk—it's about Derrick."

"Yes, I know. The others are concerned as well."

"Something has to be done—he's becoming harder and harder to handle."

"I've been talking to him. Let me deal with him."

"Henry, he's almost out of control—grabbing Novak the way he did the other night can only bring trouble if the captain finds out."

"The captain won't find out. Novak's a good soul and won't say a thing."

"Novak's also a traitor. I don't trust him."

"We don't have a choice, Louis. No one else will help us."

There were six wooden barracks and a cooking hut inside the moat. Four metal towers overlooked the barracks and a picket was stationed along each fence. The men usually worked during the day, but the river had flooded and the mill shut down and so today they were idle. Only one of the barracks was occupied and into this one went the two men. Nine other men lay in blankets on the floor of the barracks, trying to stay warm.

"What was that?" squeaked a pinched, pale face.

"The captain joyriding again," replied Henry. "Novak was driving and put the truck in the moat."

"But there was gunfire—I heard it!"

"Just the captain playing with his gun."

The pinched face sharpened, and then suddenly shrilled, "They're going to kill us! Just like the others!"

"Shut up, Derrick!" croaked one of the men.

"I'll handle this!" said Henry.

"They're going to kill us—we're doomed!"

"Shut up, you crazy fool!" countered the man again, this time sitting up.

"Be still now! I'll handle this!"

"Do something with him, Henry, we've had enough," added another.

"Come over here and talk to me, Derrick," said Henry, motioning to a corner of the barracks away from the others.

"An audience with the Pope," grinned Derrick slyly, suddenly composing himself. "Want to hear my confession, Pope?"

"Come and let's talk."

Derrick hesitated, but rose stiffly to his feet. Taking his blanket, he shuffled behind Henry to an unoccupied corner of the barracks. They sat on the dirt floor with Derrick rewrapping himself in his blanket. Henry said, "Would you like to cook for us tonight, Derrick?"

A look of wonder came over the pinched face and the small black eyes brightened. "Oh, I would like that!" said Derrick.

"Then you must be calm. Cooking takes patience."

"Yes—yes—I want to cook!"

"Good. When Novak brings the food, you shall cook. But you must be calm and quiet."

"Yes!"

"And you must not bother Novak—he's our friend."

"No!" and his black eyes suddenly darkened. "He's one of them—filthy garbage! They'll kill us! I've had a vision!"

"Derrick, get hold of yourself!"

"I've had a vision! Green grass—a breeze—blue sky; and then beyond—rocky hills—tall trees—the sun—"

"Derrick!"

"Yes! A bright, warm sun! Birds singing but—gunfire! And then—"

"Derrick Jacobs! The Honorable Derrick Jacobs of the Seventh Provincial Taxation Authority! Is the Honorable Mr. Jacobs present?"

The dark, narrowed eyes on the pinched face blinked rapidly, widened, and seemed to focus. Then a strong voice said, "Present, sir!"

"Are you available for an inquiry this evening?"

"Yes, sir!"

"We have a case involving the disposition of twelve potatoes! It is a delicate matter requiring the utmost care and discretion! There will be no harassment of the potatoes or their consort—a gentleman by the name of Novak! We will conduct ourselves appropriately during the proceedings! As an officer of the Seventh Provincial Taxation Authority, will the Honorable Mr. Jacobs be present and prepared for this undertaking?"

"Yes, sir!"

"Are you cognizant of your duties in this matter?"

"Yes, sir!"

"Will you comply with the protocol?"

"Yes, sir!"

"Then you are dismissed until this evening."

"Yes, SIR!" And the pinched face beamed proudly. Then, after thinking a moment, the beaming face added, "I will deliberate on this until the appointed time. I shall then seek the truth in this matter—the whole truth—so help me, God!"

Novak came an hour later with a dozen potatoes, some powdered broth, a partial loaf of bread, and fuel for the stove. The men had already left the barracks and were gathered in the cooking hut. Henry took the potatoes from Novak and handed them to Derrick, who was expected to quarter each one before dropping them into a large, iron pot. Instead, Derrick inspected the potatoes carefully, turning each one over and over again in his hands. The other men watched intently, their lips twitching and their jaws working in silence. Finally, Henry intervened and sliced the potatoes himself, using Novak's knife. The stove was then lit, water and broth added to the pot, and the potatoes lowered in. The men knotted tightly around the stove, warming their hands and tilting their heads forward. There then followed a peculiar hissing and wheezing as the men sniffed eagerly at the pot.

When supper was over and as the men were leaving, Henry spoke to Novak, "Thank you, Corporal."

Novak nodded.

"You will come for us in the morning, Corporal?"

Novak nodded again and then added, "As far as I know."

"I hope the captain likes his new driver."

Novak said nothing, but broke into a grin.

"Congratulations, Corporal!"

"Thank you. He doesn't like me but there aren't any other mechanics. I was worried, though. If this hadn't worked out, I was going to be shipped out."

"Trust in God. He will not fail you."

Novak laughed.

"How are things in town—I mean with the flooding?"

"I haven't heard. I suppose we'll find out in the morning."

"Corporal, I want to thank you for your help—I mean with the food and everything."

"Well, I'm sorry I had nothing extra tonight. The captain was in the mess as I was leaving." Novak glanced at his watch, "Ah—I've got to go!"

"Of course."

Novak left the hut. He followed Henry into the barracks, glanced around quickly and counted the men, and then withdrew and secured the door. He crossed a plank laid over the moat and began a muddy uphill trek toward the gates. Night had descended and the winter sky hung low and bleak. The camp lay in a valley beneath a cloud layer that hadn't lifted in weeks. Novak had not seen stars, or even the sun, for more than a month. Only blackened factory stacks pierced the grayness, standing in a silent line along the river's edge.

Despite the war, Novak remained a large man and he was sweating profusely in the damp, cool air. The guard let him through the gate, and he continued sweating all the way to the compound. There, he entered a large, rectangular building that served as the mess. The captain was inside, off in the kitchen, talking to the cook. Novak put the fuel canister away and had decided to slip out discreetly, but the captain saw him and motioned him over. Novak entered the kitchen to find the captain leaned over a half-eaten cake.

"Novak, have the truck outside my office at seven."

"Yes, sir."

"We'll take the prisoners to town to help with the flooding. Some of the factories have mud in them."

"Not the mill, then, sir?"

"The boilers have water in them. I'm not sure when it will open."

"Yes, sir. I'll be at your door at seven."

The captain then noticed Novak was sweating. He had also observed Novak's eyes darting periodically to the cake. The captain waited a minute, not yet dismissing Novak, and finally said, "Are you hungry, Novak?"

"Oh, maybe a little, sir."

"Why are you sweating?"

"Just warm, Captain. I always sweat."

"You also stink, Novak. You smell bad."

"I'm sorry, sir."

"You don't look like you're wasting away, Novak. In fact, you're fat. A pig. You should lose weight."

"I've been trying, sir."

"Try harder—you're a fat, stinking pig. You should exercise."

"Yes, sir."

The captain, who was firm and athletic, then kept at Novak for another five minutes, extolling the virtues of exercise as he finished off the cake.

\*   \*   \*

It was almost midnight when Novak closed his tool chest, stepped down from the cab of the truck, and went to his cot. He had checked the starter, but found the problem in the ignition switch itself. There were no spare parts, so he had to improvise. Lately, as the war dragged on, there seemed to be less and less materials and he had to do more and more improvising. It was one reason he had not been shipped out. His ability to patch equipment together and keep it functional had allowed him to safely stay out of the fighting.

The truck was housed in a metal shed near the center of the compound. Novak's cot was in a storage room at the rear of the shed, behind a row of shelves, the shelves stacked with miscellaneous parts scavenged from other vehicles. A squawk box had been mounted on the storage room wall and was used to summon Novak and the truck. Novak had hated the place at first—the storage room was damp and disorderly and smelled of oil and chemicals. He soon began to appreciate the privacy, though, and now pushed aside some parts on one of the shelves to reveal a photograph. This night, as on every night, he spent a few minutes quietly with this photograph of his family.

When the prisoners left for town the next morning, they were not loosely herded by Novak and the usual scattering of guards on foot. Instead, the prisoners entered town single-file between two orderly rows of troops, followed by the captain on the roof of his truck. The prisoners spent the day in a factory along the river, scooping out mud with crude shovels fashioned from sheets of corrugated roofing. That evening, after the captain returned in his truck, the men were again formed into a line and marched back to camp. This continued every day for two weeks, the prisoners cleaning out a different factory every few days.

Unlike their previous work in the mill, the factory work was cold and wet and the men couldn't stay warm. There was no boiler to get beside and the constant tramping in mud soon rendered their feet raw and bloody. Henry sensed a weakening in the men, despite Novak's daily efforts to bring more food. They also became more irritable, with an almost constant bickering setting in, though Derrick turned ever more quiet and aloof. The men became so weary and tired that Henry gave up leading their prayers at night, deciding it was better for them to sleep. Instead, he prayed out loud for them—so they could hear him as they drifted off. Finally, as the second week of factory work ended, Henry approached Novak and asked to see the captain. Novak initially protested, but finally promised to relay the request. Novak was surprised when the captain reacted favorably—the captain even saying he had been thinking of such a meeting himself.

Novak drove the captain to the barracks before dawn the next morning. "Come to order! Now!" The captain bellowed as Novak unbolted the door. There was a shuffling and popping of joints as the men rose to their feet. The captain followed Novak inside and Henry came forward to speak.

"Captain Kravitz, I asked to see you on behalf of the men."

"I will not be addressed until all prisoners rise."

Henry turned and waited as Derrick was helped from the floor. Then he continued, "Captain Kravitz, the men are weak and suffering from the cold. We could work harder with more rations and better shoes."

"There is a war going on and goods are scarce. Any surplus materials are given to those who cooperate with us."

"Captain, the men can't go on like this much longer."

"You and your men were given an opportunity to serve and refused. Your condition is a result of your own choices. Each of you still has a choice. Take the oath of allegiance and join us and this will end."

"We cannot support your movement, Captain. We believe—"

"Forget your beliefs! There is only one ideal worth pursuing—supporting the movement! We are winning! We will continue to win and overcome everyone and everything in our way! Change has come! It is time you join the change!"

"We believe that—"

"Enough! Quiet!"

The captain shifted to one side. His eyes were searching and they quickly settled on one of the men. "What's your name, prisoner?"

"Mora—Louis Mora, sir."

"You are not like these others, are you?"

"What do you mean, sir?"

"You are stronger—more fit—I've been watching you. What did you do before coming here?"

"I was a warden. At one of the game preserves."

"Which one?"

"The Third Provincial Preserve."

"Oh, yes, in the mountains along the border—very high, very beautiful. Ah! And so primitive—mule carts! Yes, I've hunted there from mule cart!"

"Hunted? You mean poached! There is no hunting allowed in the preserves! And certainly no mule carts!"

"No, Louis, I was hunting," the captain chuckled. "And hunting is allowed in the preserves! That's new—a change—and a benefit of belonging to the new order." The captain paused and went on slowly, "Don't be stubborn, Louis. Take the oath. It's your only chance—nothing else can save you."

"I'm not so sure, captain."

"Oh, really?" The captain paused a moment, thinking. Finally, he shrugged and said, "You're a fool, Louis, but suit yourself." Then, after his eyes swept the room and his face reddened, the captain's voice rose and he added, "You are all fools! There will be no additional rations, no boots, no clothes—nothing! We're at war and these are the consequences!"

The captain spun and hurried out the door. Novak hesitated, but a shout from the captain brought him scurrying along behind. The prisoners looked at Henry, and he nodded and followed. The captain and Novak were on the truck by the time Henry reached the moat, but the truck's engine was silent and Novak was fiddling with the key. The captain began to shout at Novak as Henry crossed the moat and Novak desperately worked the key. Suddenly, the truck lunged forward and the captain was thrown rearward onto the canvass cover. Novak's foot had been off the clutch when the engine finally started, and he had again left the transmission engaged.

Cursing furiously, the captain struggled off the canvass cover and back onto the cab of the truck. He noticed Henry watching him—and then other faces peering from the doorway of the barracks. Quickly, he ordered Novak to circle the moat. As the truck gained speed, the captain held tightly to his gun, his face set resolutely forward. On his third rotation of the barracks, and while the truck was still moving, the captain spun his gun abruptly and fired a short burst of shells into the roof of one of the barracks. Then, to the captain's surprise, shells continued to pour forward after his release of the trigger. Realizing the firing mechanism had jammed, the captain pivoted the gun upward. More shells were sent over the barracks until the string of shells was spent.

The captain leaned over to examine the gun as the truck slowed to a crawl. He adjusted something on the outside but soon decided the trouble was inside. Turning finally toward the barracks, he scanned them quickly. Only Henry was visible, sprawled on the ground by the moat. Once Henry began to move, the captain shouted to Novak. As the truck turned and pointed for the gates, Henry rose tentatively to his feet.

There were no injuries to the men, despite Henry counting eighteen shell holes in the walls and roof of the barracks. The men were in an uproar, except Derrick who was strangely subdued. The men's voices rose and fell sharply, with indignation and fear, but gradually quieted. Soon, the men remembered they were hungry and realized Novak had not brought their food. They also became uneasy—it was a work day and they were not being marched into town. Slowly, one by one, the men slumped to the dirt floor of the barracks and were still.

"They're going to kill us," Derrick finally whispered.

Louis, who had been reclining, sat up quickly.

"They'll kill us," Derrick repeated, a little louder.

The room was silent until Louis cleared his throat and began, "What happened to the others? I mean, there were more here before we came— Novak has mentioned it and I've seen the names carved on the beams. Henry, who was here when you arrived?"

"No one. I came with Derrick and the place was empty."

"But this is where they kept the dissidents. Where are the rest?"

"I don't know."

The room was quiet again. The men were turned toward Henry, as if expecting something. Derrick sat up and said, "Say the Mass, priest."

"Say what?" started Louis.

"Say the Mass."

Henry winced. Looking away, he said, "I promised not to."

"But you say it after we go to sleep—or when you think we are asleep."

"I was asked not to say it—and not all of you believe."

Suddenly agitated, Derrick said, "I want to see God."

"God?" retorted Louis.

"Yes. I want to see God."

"You're crazy," said Louis.

"The priest can bring God," said Derrick. The room became quiet again, the men sitting motionless on the dirt floor. Only Derrick was stirring, whispering to himself, his hands groping aimlessly in the air. Henry finally grasped Derrick's hands and folded them inside his own.

*   *   *

After a verbal lashing from the captain, Novak brought the truck to the metal shed. He repaired the ignition quickly, having diagnosed the same problem before. The gun was a more difficult project, however, and he spent the rest of the day disassembling and reassembling it several times. Finally, just as it seemed to function properly, Novak detected voices in the shed. Getting down off the truck, he went to the door but realized the voices were coming from the storage room and the squawk box adjacent to his cot. Novak was about to speak when he realized the conversation wasn't intended for him. He was eavesdropping, the squawk box having been mistakenly turned on at the other end.

"...and yes, Colonel, he was adamant. He would not cooperate."

"And what about the others?"

"Not one of them will take the oath."

"Then there are no other options. We have waited on this group longer than the others. The situation requires swift action."

"Yes, Colonel, I will take care of it."

"But without raising suspicion, Captain Kravitz. Those men are known in the provinces and we are trying to improve our standing with the people."

"Then should I handle them like the last group?"

"Don't do anything, yet. I'll come up next week and we'll handle this together. In the meantime, go easy on them. Don't let them suspect anything."

"Yes, sir, as you request. I'll be waiting for your arrival."

That evening, Novak came to the barracks at the usual time. He brought a dozen potatoes, powdered broth, and extra bread. He made an effort to appear cheerful, explaining that the captain had ordered the extra bread and seemed to regret the incident earlier that day. Novak also apologized for not coming sooner, but explained the truck and gun had to be repaired first. Then, before locking the barracks, Novak stood in the doorway and announced there would be no work in the morning.

"Why?" inquired Louis.

"The factories are cleaned out. The work there is over."

"What about the mill?"

"The captain says it will close. The boilers and generators were ruined when the water came in."

"What will we do now?"

"Uh—I don't know."

Louis squinted at Novak. Then he thrust forth a finger and blurted, "Look, Novak, what's really going on here?"

"Easy now, Louis!" broke in Henry. "I'm sure the captain will find something for us to do."

"Ah—the captain!" repeated Novak. "He must be wondering where I am! I've got to go!"

"Yes, Corporal," agreed Henry. "And tell the captain we are grateful for the bread."

When Novak had locked the barracks, Henry lay down on the floor among the men. He prayed aloud as each of them drifted off, and then got up to say Mass by himself. After Mass, he laid down and was almost asleep when there was a nudge at his shoulder.

"What do you think?"

Henry turned and saw it was Louis. "What do you mean?"

"About the captain and the bread—first he tries to kill us, then he sends us extra bread. And no work tomorrow—the second consecutive day—what's that about?"

"Providence works in strange ways. We can certainly use the rest."

"Come on, Henry. They're playing with us—this is a game."

"Don't read too much into it."

"I don't trust them—Novak or the captain."

"Then trust God. He won't fail us."

"Come on, Henry!" said Louis, rolling away.

Novak could not sleep when he lay down later that night. The voices he overheard earlier came back over and over again. He had always wondered about those confined previously at the barracks, their destinations uncertain when they left on the trains. The captain had said they were going to the western provinces, to restore areas devastated by the fighting. Suspecting now a different destination, Novak tossed uneasily in his bed.

The men in the barracks were idle the next day, and then the next as well as the next. Novak came faithfully in the mornings and evenings, bringing the men their food. The men were docile except for Louis, whose impatience grew each day. Derrick had become ever quieter, and Henry wondered if he was beginning to fail. Finally, on the evening of the fifth idle day, Novak announced that they should be ready for work in the morning.

Early the next morning, the men formed up quickly inside the moat. They expected to march into town, but instead were ordered into the back of the captain's truck. They became agitated as the guards brought out chains, and watched anxiously as they were chained to each other and then fastened to the truck. Only Louis resisted, until Henry spoke to him sharply. The captain did not take his usual position on the truck's roof, but rode inside the cab with Novak. Six guards rode with the prisoners in the back, and a jeep carrying four more guards followed behind.

For the first time since their incarceration, the men were transported beyond the camp and town. They traveled along a rural road, through a countryside that seemed lifeless and gray. Though it was already the middle of March, a winter pallor still clung to the land. It lurked as a thin shroud of fog, pressing a damp melancholy into the air. There also arose, as they traveled, a peculiar emptiness. Louis noticed it, then Henry, and eventually all the men. At first it seemed to be just a stillness, an absence of movement brought on by the lack of people and livestock along the roads and in the fields. But then came burned out barns and gutted houses, the houses surrounded by plankless fences whose posts sprouted haphazardly from the ground. Farther on, carcasses of rusted farm machinery lay spoiling in the fallow fields, and at one place they encountered a strange sort of woodland—a tract of apparent tree stumps that, upon closer inspection, turned out to be a forest of freshly planted wooden headstones. Eventually, the remains of a burned out village came into view and the truck pulled up and halted. The men were unloaded and organized into search parties and sent into the ruins. They found nothing of value during their foraging, which lasted the rest of the day. The men were sedate and worked quietly, all except Louis. He talked constantly to the guards, and Henry had to periodically intervene.

The men returned to the barracks that evening, but were idled the next day by rain. They were then brought back to the village the following morning and searched the ruins again. That evening, after returning the prisoners to the barracks, Novak drove on into the compound with the captain. Approaching the mess, they encountered a truck similar to the captain's, but newer and in better condition. Before Novak could stop completely, the captain had slipped out of the cab.

Lagging behind, Novak entered the mess through the kitchen. Working quickly, he had already collected the things necessary for the prisoners' supper when the captain noticed him. Called into the dining hall, Novak found the captain seated across the table from a large, fleshy colonel. A cake sat between them and the colonel was eating it. Surrounding the colonel was a detachment of unfamiliar troops, who grinned at Novak as he approached.

"Colonel Savoy, this is my driver—Corporal Novak. Best damned mechanic in the province! I wish he could drive, though—" began the captain, stopping to cackle and poke Novak in the ribs.

"Corporal, the captain and I have selected you for a special mission," the colonel began casually. "It's confidential for security reasons, but things will become obvious as we go along. It will be important for you to perform well and follow instructions."

"Yes, sir."

The captain then added, "It's set for tomorrow. Bring the truck at seven and make sure it's fueled. Also, load extra ammo cans for the gun. We'll go ahead in our own truck and the colonel will join us later. The cook is preparing some food to take along. That is all. Go and finish what you were doing."

"Yes, sir."

Novak brought a dozen potatoes, powdered broth, and six onions to the cooking hut. Henry prepared the food, the stove was lit, and the men gathered closely around the pot. When the cooking was finished and after Henry had said the blessing, Derrick rose unexpectantly. He circled the cluster of men and came to Henry. His eyes were bright and shining as he said in a clear voice, "I want to go to confession, priest. I want forgiveness."

Startled, Henry replied, "Okay, Derrick." Then he added, "But after we eat."

"No, right now."

"Right now?"

"It can't wait. And after—I mean, later tonight—I want to stay up for Mass."

"Please, Derrick—" Louis began.

"I'll be glad to hear your confession, Derrick," said Henry, standing quickly. "Come with me."

They went out of the cooking hut and into the barracks. In half an hour, they returned. The others had finished eating and Novak was gathering up things to leave. Derrick ate quickly and left, and soon only Henry and Novak remained in the hut.

"I didn't know you were a priest," said Novak, abruptly.

"Yes."

"How long?"

"This is my twenty-third year."

Novak was about to continue but stopped. Henry waited, then inquired, "Novak, what faith are you?"

"Eastern Rite—sort of. Actually, I don't practice anything right now."

"I see." Henry was thoughtful for a moment. Then he said, "Corporal, why did you take the oath?"

Novak, who had bent over the stove, rose and turned to face the priest, "I have a family—six children. I don't see them often, but they're my whole life. It's all I care about—more than myself."

"How are they doing?"

"They aren't starving, but it's hard. Hard on everyone. I have two small boys—seven and four. I see them every few months for a day or so. This civil war is hell. It's ruined everything."

"Yes, almost everything," agreed Henry.

Novak went on, "It's not like the captain says. There is nothing for us common people—even for those who comply. They promised us things but they take it all for themselves—the captain and those like him. They promised change, but it is worse now than before the war."

"I know." There was a short silence, and then Henry inquired evenly, "Corporal, whatever happened to the other men who were here—the ones before us?"

Novak felt fortunate he was now turned toward the door. After a moment to gather himself, he carefully replied, "They went to the western provinces—sent as part of the reconstruction effort. They were sent to areas devastated by the fighting."

"I see. Well, Corporal, I won't hold you up any longer. It's about time for you to go."

"Please, one final thing—" said Novak, turning toward Henry.

"Yes?"

"Please, remember me in your prayers. And my family—I ask for mercy."

"You are already in my prayers. And I will pray for your family."

"Thank you. These are dark times."

Henry blinked and tilted his head to the side. He noticed a sadness in Novak's voice that he hadn't detected before. Novak remained standing before him, as if expecting something. Finally, Henry reached out and touched Novak gently on the shoulder. "Be at peace," Henry said. "May God bless you."

Novak exhaled sharply, saying, "Thank you."

Novak followed Henry to the barracks, secured the barracks door, and then returned to the compound. Relieved to find the mess empty, he returned the cooking equipment to the place it was stored. As he was leaving through the rear door of the kitchen, he spotted a row of four cakes on top of one of the ovens. Novak went over and examined them, sniffing furtively. The cakes had been set out to cool and Novak could feel their warmth on his face. Then, after glancing about nervously, he left the kitchen and went to the metal shed. He loaded several ammunition cans before driving the truck out for fuel. When he returned, he made an inspection of the vehicle. Later, he tossed on his cot, finding it difficult to lie still. Finally, he got up to move aside equipment on one of the shelves to look at the photograph of his family.

* * *

Henry awoke the following morning while it was still dark. He remained stretched out on the floor for several minutes, listening to the occasional creak and murmur from the men. When Henry sat up, he noticed Derrick was gone. Glancing around quickly, Henry found him at a corner of the barracks where his face seemed to be pressed closely to the wall. Henry rose quietly and went over and stood behind him. Derrick sat cross-legged with his face just an inch or two from the boards. He had found a wide split in the wood and was staring outside.

"What do you see, Derrick?" There was no response and no movement.

"Derrick, what do you see?" Henry repeated in a low voice. Still there was no response. Henry then squat down beside Derrick and peered out through the split in the boards. A dense fog had settled in and little was visible, only vague silhouettes in a shifting mist. There also was a sweet, burning odor that reminded Henry of diesel fuel. Finally, Henry again inquired, "What are you looking at, Derrick?"

"Lord have mercy," Derrick said softly.

"What?"

"Say, 'Lord have mercy'," Derrick said.

Henry was silent.

"Say, 'Lord have mercy'," repeated Derrick, his voice rising.

"Lord have mercy," Henry responded, keeping his own voice low.

"Christ have mercy."

"Christ have mercy," Henry repeated.

"Lord have mercy."

"Lord have mercy," Henry repeated.

"Glory to God in the highest—" Derrick intoned, and then he was quiet. After a minute or so, he turned and faced Henry and with his small, black eyes burning in the darkness, he said, "'How long will they set upon a man and altogether beat him down—as though he were a sagging fence, a battered wall?'"

"You quote scripture."

Derrick nodded.

"I'll finish the passage for you: 'Only in God is our soul at rest—from Him comes our salvation. He only is our rock and our salvation, our stronghold—we shall not be disturbed at all. One thing God said—these things I have heard—that all power belongs to God, Who renders to everyone according to his deeds.'"

"'According to his deeds,'" Derrick repeated. Then, he went on, "Remember what you said at confession last night—about the peacemakers and the poor in spirit? Could you repeat it?"

Henry repeated the verses from the previous night.

"Those verses—I've known most of them since I was a child. But others—I'd forgotten them—the parts about blessing those who hate you, returning good for evil. They're hard words, Henry. Harder than I thought."

"Yes, they are."

"It's hard, Henry—hard to give it up."

"Yes. But we can only do what we can do. When we can't do it any longer, give it to God."

"Yes, you are right. It's taken me a long time to see it."

"Ask for grace and a pure heart, Derrick, free of evil and hatred. Then you will see God."

"Yes."

There then came an unexpected grinding of gears and from out of the fog emerged the captain's truck. Derrick and Henry watched through the boards as the vehicle drew up. The captain dismounted and then both he and Novak approached the barracks.

"Wake up! Come to order!" bellowed the captain, as Novak unlocked the door. Novak and the captain had arrived earlier than usual, and most of the men were barely awake. "Form a line and prepare for loading!"

The men grumbled as they stirred and shuffled and rose to form up. As they exited the barracks, the captain said, "There will be food later if you don't complain. There is a lot to do today."

The men were loaded and chained, and then the truck pulled away. It passed up through the iron gates and on into the compound. Despite the fog and lingering darkness, Henry noticed a truck similar to the captain's at the mess. As they were leaving the compound, Henry turned to look again for this truck but his attention was claimed by something else. One of the blackened factory stacks was sending up a peculiar blue, smoky vapor. Turning up the valley from the camp, Henry realized the stack belonged to the mill and the sweet, burning odor came from firing of the generators inside.

The truck followed the same rural road as before. The fog clung close to the ground, obscuring the countryside as they rolled along. After passing the village where they worked previously, the truck went on several more miles before halting at a second village. This second village was also gutted and burned and, once again, the men were grouped into search parties and sent into the ruins.

In the remains of a building that fronted the town square, in what must have been a shop or mercantile, Louis broke through the flooring and landed upright in a small cellar. The cellar was empty but as he climbed out, Louis noticed a narrow crawl space between the cellar and the floor. Reaching in, Louis touched something and then carefully pulled out a bottle. Quickly, Louis pulled out six more bottles before opening and tasting the first. A group of prisoners gathered above him, attracting two of the guards. Louis had consumed half of the first bottle when the guards began shouting and pointing. A sea of arms surged into the hole, prompting a volley of shells overhead. Everyone froze as Novak inched the truck toward them with the captain on the roof.

"What's going on here?" demanded the captain.

"We've found some wine!" exclaimed one of the guards. Then, pointing to Louis, he continued, "And this swine is drinking it!"

"Let me see what you have!"

Louis raised the open bottle through the hole in the floor and a guard took it and passed it up to the captain. The captain smelled it, looked inside the bottle, and then poured a bit out on the roof of the truck. It was a deep, purple wine.

"There's more," said one of the guards.

"Bring up the rest," said the captain. "And be careful with it!"

"We should have some—I found it!" demanded Louis.

"Hand up the bottles and we'll see."

Wine on an empty stomach had already begun to make Louis tipsy, but still he guided each bottle up carefully through the hole. Only Henry, and then the captain, noticed a second truck approach from the rear.

"Ah! We have visitors," said the captain, and he got down off the roof of his truck. Grasping two unopened wine bottles, the captain walked to the second truck. All eyes followed as he stepped up on the running board and spoke to the two inside. Soon, there was laughing from the cab. The captain passed the two bottles inside and returned to reclaim the already opened one.

"We're done here," the captain announced. "There's other work to do. Load up and let's go!"

Louis, now partly emerged from the cellar, complained, "What about the wine? We should get some."

"Not now," said the captain.

"Not now?—I found it! We should get some!" shouted Louis.

"Quiet, you fool!" said the captain, drawing closer.

"You're the fool—filthy pig!"

Before Henry could intervene, the captain swung the already opened wine bottle and brought it down solidly on Louis' head. The bottle shattered, and Louis dropped backwards into the cellar. Grinning, the captain turned to Henry and gestured toward the opening. "Get him out of there," commanded the captain.

As everyone waited, Henry descended into the cellar with Derrick. Together they pushed Louis up though the opening, and then two other prisoners carried Louis toward the trucks. Once all the men were gathered and formed up at the trucks, the colonel emerged from the second truck and the captain introduced him. Then the captain split the prisoners into two groups; one group went with the captain and the other with the colonel in the second truck.

The two trucks left the village with the captain's truck in the lead. The captain rode up front with Novak, as Louis lay unconscious in back against the rear gate. Henry kneeled beside Louis, plucking shards of glass from his scalp. At intervals as they traveled, Henry gazed quietly at the landscape outside. Gradually, the empty fields and pastures passed into damp and somber woodlands. Though the fog finally lifted, the cloud sheet that seemed to hover perpetually overhead now seemed to press down heavier than before.

After an hour of woods and winding roadway, the valley narrowed sharply. Rounding a bend, the road turned back on itself and began to climb steeply. After ascending for three or four miles, the road widened and the trucks halted along the crest of a ridge. From the rear of the truck, Henry glimpsed the valley floor far below. The captain slipped out of the cab to confer with the colonel. Henry noticed both men were drinking and had taken on a jocular mood.

The trucks set off again. They soon intersected the cloud layer hovering over the valley and the air turned wet and cold. A damp eeriness set in as the trucks probed cautiously through the mist. The prisoners in the captain's truck were silent, huddled against the chill. In his mirror, Novak noticed the colonel's truck gradually falling behind until soon it had dropped back, out of sight, into the grayness. The road eventually flattened, but then began to curve sharply through a series of bends. At one place the truck almost left the road, encountering a sheen of ice that slid the vehicle toward the edge. Correcting the truck's trajectory, Novak noticed the captain rising abruptly from his seat. For an instant, the captain had glimpsed the almost vertical descent from the roadway's edge.

After several miles of bends and turns, the road straightened onto a long, steep grade. At the top of the grade, the truck emerged abruptly from the clouds and leveled off, entering bright, warm sunlight. Shading his eyes, Novak braked the truck sharply. The captain buried his face in his arms and cursed. Beneath the truck's canvass cover, the prisoners and guards grimaced and blinked rapidly at each other.

The truck had climbed onto the edge of a flat, grassy plateau. With the sunlight had come a burst of color, and ahead of the truck, extending to a range of mountains on the horizon, spread an immense meadow of green. The sky, no longer dull and gray, curved overhead in a canopy of blue. Directly above them, round and burnished, was the sun throwing off bright yellow beams. Behind the truck, a sea of cloud stretched from the lip of the plateau toward the other horizon. The top of this gray layer was flat and almost level with the surface of the plateau. The gray seemed to be motionless, except for a tumbling and churning along the edges. There was a slight breeze, and occasionally a wisp or eddy of gray would detach from the cloud layer and dart rapidly onto the meadow. These quickly vanished, consumed by the warmth and light of the plateau.

The truck remained stationary for several minutes. The men in the rear began to whisper and shift about, stirred by their new surroundings. The captain soon climbed on top of the cab and ordered Novak onward, and the truck began across the plateau. The road pointed toward the range of mountains beyond the grassy plain.

They had gone less than a mile when the truck suddenly halted after a shout from the captain. Unexpectedly, a cart drawn by a mule approached from the other direction. An old man held the reins and waved briefly as he passed. The captain waved and shouted something before ordering Novak on. The men in back of the truck watched the cart grow smaller as it drew away.

The truck proceeded another two or three miles. The captain shifted about on the roof, more active than before. As the truck reached the top of a small knoll, the captain again ordered Novak to a stop. Novak pulled up just beyond the crest of the knoll, where the road sloped slightly forward, and shut off the engine. To keep the truck from rolling, Novak then set the transmission in reverse. All was quiet for a few minutes, though the captain shuffled about on the roof.

"Everyone out!" the captain finally shouted. "There's work to be done!"

The men were unchained and began climbing out of the truck. As Henry stepped down, he glanced about quickly, wondering what sort of work they would do.

"Guards, at your stations! Corporal Novak—get the prisoners some food!"

The food was being transported in a large metal box. Novak and three of the guards placed the box on the side of the road about thirty yards in front of the truck. The prisoners gathered there, except for Henry, who waited at the back of the truck beside Louis.

"What are you waiting for?" barked the captain at Henry.

"He's moving—waking up," said Henry, pointing to Louis in the back of the truck. "He needs some water."

"Corporal Novak, get some water."

"Yes, Captain."

Henry wet a rag from his pocket and wiped at the crust of blood and wine that had dried on Louis' face. In a few minutes, Louis managed to sit up on the truck's rear gate. Looking around blankly, he inquired, "Where are we?"

"I'm not sure," said Henry. "We've been traveling for more than three hours."

"What are we doing here?"

"I'm not sure of that either. Sit here a bit until you're ready to walk—there's some food for us."

As he waited with Louis, Henry scanned the grassy knoll. The place where they stopped was a raised area, providing a good view all around. The plateau seemed almost featureless, except for the endless grasses. A wandering breeze seemed to shift aimlessly, pushing a few small, singing birds about in the current. Henry eventually spotted a small barn about a mile ahead, and he was reminded of the cart that passed earlier. Turning around, Henry scanned along the edge of the plateau, but the cart was gone. He presumed it had descended the road into the clouds. It occurred to Henry that the second truck was very slow, not yet having appeared on the plateau.

"Enjoy your nap?" said the captain suddenly, having pivoted toward them from his perch on the cab of the truck.

Louis didn't respond, so Henry spoke instead, "He's coming around, Captain. Just another minute or so."

"Good. I've got something to show him."

"What's he talking about?" said Louis, softly.

Henry shrugged. Then the captain grinned and said, "You missed something while you napped. We passed a mule cart—the only traffic the whole way. When was the last time you saw one of those?"

"Mule carts are still used—mostly to haul wood—I've seen them over by—" Louis began. Suddenly, he rose off the rear gate and turned around. Ahead of the truck, a few miles in the distance, a row of tall peaks filled the horizon. Recognizing them, Louis said, "We're near one of the game preserves!"

"Correct!"

"Why are we here?" probed Henry.

"Ah," the captain crowed, "there's a job to do!"

"What kind of job?"

"You'll find out soon enough. We'll start as soon as—uh—the colonel arrives." Then the captain laughed nervously, glanced quickly over Henry and Louis toward the edge of the plateau, and added, "It seems he's fallen behind. I thought he would be here by now. You should get some food before it's all gone."

Henry and Louis started walking. The guards were assembled along the steel bulwark attached to the front of the truck, rifles over their shoulders, passing opened bottles of wine. Thirty yards ahead, the other prisoners were congregated around the food box, glutting themselves. Louis joined in, but Henry paused first to pray and discreetly bless the food. Henry then picked through the food box, past two cakes and some dried meat, until he found a loaf of bread. He was about to break it when he noticed Novak lifting a can of ammunition onto the roof of the truck. The captain positioned the can on top of one already there, and began to feed a belt of shells into his gun. Still holding the loaf, Henry inched toward Louis.

"Something's wrong," whispered Henry.

"What?" squawked Louis, tearing at his food.

"Shhh! Be quiet!"

Louis stopped chewing and said, "What the hell is wrong with you, Henry?"

"Look at the captain—now!" The captain was bent over, making an adjustment to his gun.

"Oh no!"

"Don't panic—just keep eating!"

"The bastard's going to kill us—right here!"

"Just eat! I have an idea!"

"Let's storm them, Henry—we're finished anyway!"

Henry grabbed Louis' arm and turned him around. In the same movement, he reached down and bent back two of Louis' fingers. Louis would have screamed but there was food in his mouth and, instead, he began coughing. The guards looked over and the captain, continuing to fumble with his gun, glanced up. Henry waited until the captain was again preoccupied and the guards went back to drinking. Then, in a low voice, he spoke tersely to Louis, "We have a chance, but you must do as I say!"

"There's no chance—we're good as dead!"

"Listen to me! There are only four guards, plus Novak and the captain."

"We should rush them, Henry."

"No! We start walking—slowly—down the road. Out of range of the captain's gun. The guards have been drinking—they'll be slow to react."

"You're crazy. It won't work."

"It will work—have faith—just move toward the others."

The other prisoners were still eating but had slowed their pace. Edging up next to them, Henry warned, "Start walking—slowly! Don't ask why—just move—now! When Louis gives the word—run! Spread out and run!" The men hesitated, but the urgency in Henry's voice started them on their way.

"Where are they going!" one of the guards exclaimed.

The captain looked up quickly from his gun and barked, "Halt! Halt!"

The prisoners stopped. Henry volunteered, "We're moving around a bit so our food can settle. We're just about ready to work."

"Stay where you are!" commanded the captain.

Henry then whispered to Louis, "I'll start back toward the captain. When you see a chance—run!"

"What are you doing?" hissed Louis.

"Just do as I say."

As Henry started toward the truck, the guards took their rifles from their shoulders. The captain stood erect at his gun, and pointed it at Henry. Henry stopped at the food box to collect himself. Then, confronting the captain and the guards, he raised his arms and exclaimed, "Blessed be God for ever—may the Lord be with you!"

The captain reddened and said, "Go to hell!"

"Lift up your hearts—lift your hearts to the Lord!"

"Shut up, you fool!"

"It is right to give him thanks and praise!"

"Shut up, fool!"

"Holy, holy is our Lord! Heaven and earth are full of his glory! Blessed is he who comes in the name of the Lord! Praise his name!"

"Enough, damn it! You made a promise, priest—a bargain! No God! No religion! None of it—remember?"

Henry paused for several seconds. Then, in a lowered voice, he replied, "Do you intend to keep your part of the bargain?"

The captain was startled. Then he grinned and laughed, "Neither of us is very good at promises, eh?"

"I have been praying for you, Captain."

"Praying for me? You are very stupid, priest—you and your friends. Your homes are destroyed, property confiscated, your families have fled or are dead. Everything sacrificed!"

"Please, it is not too late—"

"Shut up!"

"You do not know what you are doing—"

"Captain!" interrupted one of the guards, "They're getting away!"

The captain glanced beyond Henry and saw the other prisoners running down the road. Quickly leveling his gun, he leaned over and shouted to Novak, "Let's go, Corporal! Move it!"

The guards climbed onto the front of the truck. They stood upright, in a narrow space between the radiator and the steel bulwark attached to the bumper, aiming their rifles unsteadily. Inside the cab, Novak had inserted the key. When he turned it, the truck wouldn't start.

"Let's go! Now!" bellowed the captain.

"I'm trying, sir."

"Go! Go!"

"It's the ignition again, sir—"

"What!"

"It won't start—I can't help it, sir."

"You dumb bastard! You dumb, stupid bastard! Get it started, right now!"

"I'm trying!"

"Damn it, Novak—they're getting away!"

The guards began to fire their rifles. The prisoners had left the road and were now spreading out through the meadow. Henry ducked down behind the metal box as Novak, inside the truck, continued to work the key. The captain stomped furiously on the truck's roof, the bumping causing Novak's foot to slip off the clutch. Then the engine abruptly fired.

Despite his rage, the captain had not forgotten Novak's tendency to start with the transmission engaged. Expecting the truck to lurch suddenly, the captain had braced himself at his gun. Unlike previous occasions, though, the transmission was set in reverse gear and so the truck jumped rearward instead of ahead. The jolt flung the guards forward, over the steel bulwark, and onto the road. The captain also was pitched forward, and would have landed on the engine cover, except that his hands became tangled in the grips of his gun. Somersaulted onto his back across the vertical gun guards, his legs lay flopped along the barrel and snout of his gun. His twisted fingers activated the trigger and, suddenly, a roar of shells bore into his legs and thighs. The gun surged at first, then hesitated, and then surged again. This was repeated several times, and at each hesitation the gun's recoil caused the captain to pitch and toss, jerking the gun about. As the gun swung erratically, it spewed a fountain of shells that swept through the guards. Though the captain's hands finally fell away from the grips and the trigger, it wasn't until after the entire can of shells passed through the gun that there came an eerie silence.

In the quiet that followed, Henry lay motionless on the edge of the road. He waited carefully for any sound or movement, but finally peered from behind the box. The guards lay spread out in front of him, motionless on the pavement. The captain was dismembered, and parts of him littered the hood and roof of the truck. In a corner of the windshield, through the only glass not bathed in blood and fragments of flesh, Novak was staring blankly ahead.

\*   \*   \*

In the cloud layer below the plateau, at the place where the road from the valley flattened and weaved sharply through a series of curves, the colonel's truck sat immobilized. A sheen of ice had sent the truck sliding through a curve, and the truck now sat sideways across the road with its front wheels sunk solidly in a ditch on the inside of the curve. The prisoners had been told to dismount and were now lined up along the front bumper, to give the truck a push. The guards and the colonel remained on the truck, huddled against the gray and cold. The corporal who did the driving for the colonel began to bark out a cadence, and the prisoners began to rock the truck back and forth. On the fifth push, the front tires rose out of the ditch and the truck began to roll backwards.

The road sloped in such a way that when the corporal applied the brakes, the truck continued backwards, sliding on the sheen of ice. In a matter of seconds, the truck vanished over the edge of the road. There was then a few more seconds of silence, followed by a muffled explosion. When the astonished prisoners peered over the side of the road, all they could see was swirling mist.

The prisoners stood gaping at each other as a mule cart suddenly rounded the bend of the road. The men were nearly overrun, but the cart pulled up sharply. Derrick spoke to the old man at the reins, who thrust his thumb rearward in the direction of the plateau. The old man intended to proceed, but Derrick and the others boarded the cart. After a brief protest, the old man turned the cart around and began his way back up toward the plateau.

On the plateau, Novak sat stoically in the truck as Henry approached, the engine idling smoothly. Already, Henry had made a quick examination of the guards and found no survivors. Stepping up on the truck's running board, Henry heard a shout from behind and turned to see Louis striding through the grasses. Henry turned again toward Novak, reached past him into the cab, and switched off the truck's engine.

"My God, what happened?" said Louis.

"The captain had an accident," Henry understated.

"The guards?"

"All dead," Henry summarized quickly. "Where are the others?"

"We're all to meet at the barn up ahead," and Louis pointed toward the structure Henry noticed earlier. "I told them to wait half an hour and then go on if I didn't come."

"Anyone hurt?"

"I don't think so."

"Thank God," said Henry, turning and glancing behind the truck toward the edge of the plateau.

Abruptly, Louis grasped Henry's arm and spoke excitedly, "Henry, I know this country! There's a back road to the border—through the mountains—just ahead! The border is less than twenty miles away!"

"Look behind us!"

Louis turned, following Henry's gaze toward the edge of the plateau. Something had emerged from the clouds and was coming toward them on the road.

"We'd better get down."

"I'll get some guns," said Louis.

Henry left the road and crept off into the meadow. Louis soon followed and both lay down in the grass fifty yards or so from the road. Novak remained in the truck, staring straight ahead. Louis had grabbed the two nearest rifles and given one to Henry. Henry's gun was a short-barreled shotgun and Louis noticed Henry seemed to handle it with apparent familiarity. Henry opened the chamber and found it still contained two cartridges—both rubber shot with a light charge. It apparently had not been fired. "This is a riot gun," Henry said to himself out loud.

There then followed several minutes of waiting and watching. Finally, Louis turned to Henry and whispered, "Mule cart." Slowing cautiously as it approached the truck on the knoll, the cart finally stopped. With a grunt of recognition, Louis rose from the grass and shouted, "Over here! Derrick! Over here!"

After a brief reunion, the cleanup began. The guards were pulled off the road and into the grass. The captain's larger parts were swept off the cab and hood using a broom Novak kept behind the seat, and then the rest of the captain was hosed away with water from one of the truck's holding tanks. After the metal food box was loaded into the back, Louis shoved Novak aside on the seat of the truck and drove Henry and the other men up to the barn, the mule cart following behind.

Soon, all the men were reassembled on the side of the barn, grinning and slapping each other on the back. Then Louis slipped away from the others and took a rifle to the door of the truck. "Come out of there," he said to Novak. "Easy now."

Novak remained seated, staring straight ahead. Louis opened the door, his voice rising, and repeated, "Come on out!"

Novak still didn't move. Louis then sprang up onto the running board of the truck and slammed the butt of his rifle into the side of Novak's head. Novak slumped over, but Louis thrust his rifle again and again. Finally, as Louis struggled to bring the barrel of his gun around in the cramped cab of the truck, Novak yelled out.

It took Derrick and Henry both to pull Louis from the cab of the truck. The three of them then thrashed around on the gravel surface beside the barn, until Louis was finally subdued. "Let's finish him!" screamed Louis, grappling for the rifle that Derrick finally hurled into the grass.

"Listen to yourself—what are you saying?"

"Kill him!"

"It's over, Louis—"

"He's mine! I'll kill the fat pig!"

"Stop it, Louis!" said Henry, finally grasping Louis' hair and forcing his face to meet his.

Louis went limp, still in the grasp of Henry and Derrick. He then sulked quietly until finally, almost serenely, Louis said, "He should die."

"Why do you say that?" asked Derrick.

"They tried to kill us—he was in on it."

"But we were spared," broke in Henry.

"He was part of it."

"We're alive, Louis. The Lord is merciful."

"Novak doesn't deserve mercy."

"The Lord has mercy for all of us—even Novak."

Louis shuddered. He remained sitting on the gravel, listless and quiet, until he began to weep.

Leaving Louis with Derrick, Henry went and found Novak lying across the seat of the truck. His hands were bloody and covered his face. "I'm sorry—I'm sorry," he kept repeating, sobbing to himself.

"How is he?" Henry asked one of the men who was looking after him.

"His face is a mess—but I don't think it's serious."

Novak sat up at the sound of Henry's voice. He lowered his hands, blinking through the blood. Henry took the rag he had used previously on Louis and asked one of the other men to wet it. As he wiped off Novak's face with the rag, Henry said, "You're cut up and it looks like your nose is broken. I apologize. I'll see to it that none of the others harm you."

Novak grunted. Derrick then appeared at the door of the truck with the old man who drove the cart. The old man said, "You must go—they have patrols."

Looking at Derrick, Henry said, "Let's load up. Louis knows the way—is he ready to travel?"

"I think so," said Derrick.

Facing Novak, Henry said, "You are free to join us, but we must leave now."

Novak did not respond. Henry was about to repeat himself, but Novak said, "My family—what about my family? They'll be killed if I go."

Hesitating, Derrick finally said, "You can't go back—how will you explain what happened here?"

Novak said nothing, but eased himself slowly out of the cab and teetered toward the front of the truck. He leaned against the steel bulwark, facing the truck's radiator, flanked by Derrick and Henry. Behind the truck, the sun had fallen toward the horizon and was almost touching the clouds. Glancing up, Derrick realized it would be dark soon. Novak finally said, "I don't know what to do—I can't leave my family. They'll be killed."

Henry had been thinking. He started toward the cab of the truck, going to the passenger's side. Louis was now in the driver's seat, resting with his eyes closed. Henry removed the short-barreled shotgun that he earlier placed under the seat. He opened the chamber and removed one of the two cartridges, and then returned to the front of the truck. Leveling the barrel several feet from Novak's backside, he pulled the trigger. There was a muffled explosion and Novak fell forward, into the bulwark. Then Novak collapsed to the ground, groaning and writhing. Henry lowered the shotgun, walked back to the cab, and slid it again under the seat.

"What have you done?" Derrick shrieked.

"Get some rags and wrap him up—we need to go," Henry said calmly.

"Are you crazy, Henry?"

"Don't stand there and let him bleed to death—do what I told you. And you there—" Henry motioned to the old man now seated in his cart, "—can you carry this man to a doctor?"

The old man shrugged and nodded.

Everyone was now gathered around Novak. Even Louis had climbed down from the truck and was standing with the others. "What's this about, Henry?" said Louis.

"Novak was caught in an ambush—don't you see?" as Henry pointed to Novak. "He was shot from behind! Even so, he defended his captain bravely—look at his bashed-in face! The sole survivor—a hero! And this kind old man—" Henry now gestured to the driver of the cart, "—found him left for dead on the road." Henry paused a moment, grinning broadly.

"Of course—I think that might work," said one of the men.

"Load him onto the cart—we need to go," ordered Henry.

"Just like that?" said Derrick. "He won't make it—I think he's in shock—look at him."

Novak lay shaking on the ground. Henry looked at Novak, then at Derrick and Louis, and finally at the rest of the men. Then Henry said, "I have a solution—go ahead and load him into the cart." While Novak was being moved, Henry went to the metal box in the back of the truck. Rummaging inside, he pulled out an empty can and a partial loaf of bread. Coming to the front of the truck, he pried loose a wine bottle that one of the guards had jammed into the grating protecting the radiator. After pouring some wine into the can, Henry set the can and the bread on the floor of the cart beside Novak. Gathering the men around him, Henry signed himself and kneeled, indicating the men should do likewise. He began to pray silently, then audibly, until finally he took the bread, raised and broke it, and said, "Take this, all of you, and eat it: this is my body which will be given up for you." And several moments later, he raised the can and continued, "Take this, all of you, and drink from it: this is the cup of my blood—" Then, after praying a while longer, Henry raised the bread and the can and said, "Behold the Lamb of God—behold him who takes away the sin of the world—"

Most of the men, initially perplexed, were now prostrate on the ground. Three of the men hesitated and remained standing with Louis, not sure what to do. Derrick fainted and slumped backwards, where Louis caught him and laid him out gently on the gravel. Most of the men then got up and surged toward Henry, their jostling pushing Louis and the other three men toward the cart. Derrick revived quickly, and rose to follow the larger group of men. Soon, Henry approached the cart and said, "Do you wish to receive?"

Novak, reclining uncomfortably but with his eyes wide open, said, "I am not worthy."

Louis added, "Nor am I. I wanted to kill him," and he pointed at Novak.

"None of us are worthy. Are you repentant?"

"Yes," Novak and Louis said together.

"Do you want to be healed? Do you want to change? If so, then receive His Body!"

One of the three other men then said, "Henry, you know we are Christian—but not of your faith. This is not one of our customs."

"Do you believe in Jesus?" inquired Henry.

"Yes, of course."

"Do you want his life in you?"

"Yes—"

"Then receive—and be changed."

Ten minutes later, the truck was readied and the men seated in back. Henry sat up front in the cab with Louis, and Henry began to sing. Novak watched as the truck pulled away, merging gradually into the oncoming night. Stars began to blink as the breeze strengthened, and the grasses rolled and tossed. Novak wanted to linger a while longer on the plateau, but with a snap of the reins, the old man started the mule cart off with a lurch. Novak had been in pain, but was now feeling better. He had been left the last of the wine, and was sipping slowly from the bottle. Novak was content as the cart descended into the clouds from the plateau.

www.ingramcontent.com/pod-product-compliance
Lightning Source LLC
Chambersburg PA
CBHW071350170626
46811CB00003B/1070